"Not Fair…" Lips. "I Don' Let Alone ... Means…"

"Harres…Harres Aal Shalaan…"

She suddenly gasped then pushed away.

He stared down at her, all his being rioting, needing her back against him, her lips crushed beneath his, her heat enveloping his suddenly chilled body.

She gaped up at him.

Then she finally rasped, "You're an Aal Shalaan?"

Harres nodded, already acutely sorry that he'd told her.

Now it would end, the spontaneity of the attraction that had exploded into life between them.

Now that he'd told her who he was, nothing could ever be the same.

Dear Reader,

I can't tell you how I much I loved writing Harres and Talia's story. But wait, I can! And I'm here to do so.

This story was one I'd longed to write. A true desert romance. Not one taking place in Zohayd's palaces among luxury and man-made grandeur, with the only threats being the insidious royal conspiracies and political intrigue, but one out there in the desert, where nature is the ultimate enchantment and enemy, and where constant danger to the hero's and heroine's lives and hearts is omnipresent.

It was an adrenaline rush to write every word, from the moment Harres burst in to save Talia, to every moment of their journey back to safety as peril and passion rose to unmanageable levels. That journey ended only for another to begin—one of tumultuous surrender to their desires—in the sanctuary of an oasis whose beauty and magic deepened every meaning and sharpened each sensation. Then came the return to the metaphorical royal jungle, where no one was an ally of their bond and their enemies were ready with brutal tests to force it to the breaking point. Even I was wondering how their love would survive!

So now I've told you how much I adored writing this story! I can only hope you enjoy it as much.

Thank you so much for reading, and I'm always eager to hear from readers. Please contact me at oliviagates@gmail.com and visit me at www.oliviagates.com. I'd love it if you friend me on Facebook or follow me on Twitter.

Happy reading!

Olivia

OLIVIA GATES

TO TEMPT A SHEIKH

Silhouette®

Desire

Published by Silhouette Books

America's Publisher of Contemporary Romance

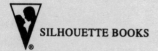 **SILHOUETTE BOOKS**

ISBN-13: 978-0-373-73082-7

Recycling programs for this product may not exist in your area.

TO TEMPT A SHEIKH

Copyright © 2011 by Olivia Gates

All rights reserved. Except for use in any review, the reproduction or utilization of this work in whole or in part in any form by any electronic, mechanical or other means, now known or hereafter invented, including xerography, photocopying and recording, or in any information storage or retrieval system, is forbidden without the written permission of the editorial office, Silhouette Books, 233 Broadway, New York, NY 10279 U.S.A.

This is a work of fiction. Names, characters, places and incidents are either the product of the author's imagination or are used fictitiously, and any resemblance to actual persons, living or dead, business establishments, events or locales is entirely coincidental.

This edition published by arrangement with Harlequin Books S.A.

For questions and comments about the quality of this book please contact us at Customer_eCare@Harlequin.ca.

® and TM are trademarks of Harlequin Books S.A., used under license. Trademarks indicated with ® are registered in the United States Patent and Trademark Office, the Canadian Trade Marks Office and in other countries.

Visit Silhouette Books at www.eHarlequin.com

Printed in U.S.A.

OLIVIA GATES

has always pursued creative passions like singing and handicrafts. She still does, but only one of her passions grew gratifying enough, consuming enough, to become an ongoing career—writing.

She is most fulfilled when she is creating worlds and conflicts for her characters, then exploring and untangling them bit by bit, sharing her protagonists' every heart-wrenching heartache and hope, their every heart-pounding doubt and trial, until she leads them to an indisputably earned and gloriously satisfying happy ending.

When she's not writing, she is a doctor, a wife to her own alpha male and a mother to one brilliant girl and one demanding Angora cat. Visit Olivia at www.oliviagates.com.

To my mother.
No words can describe how relieved I am
that the worst is over.
Here's to many, many more books with us together.

One

Harres Aal Shalaan tightened his shroud, narrowing the opening across his eyes to a slit. He didn't need more than that to monitor his target.

The midnight wind buffeted him, pelted him with sand as he stilled once more, flattened himself at the uppermost edge of the dune. His cloth-smothered breathing still rivaled the wind's hubbub across the endlessness of the desert in his ears.

He absently reached for his sand car much as he would have his prized horse. The vehicle wasn't there. He'd left it behind over two miles away. Any closer and the engine noise would have transmitted across this sound-hurling landscape. Ideally, he would have dragged it to this vantage point, but that would have slowed him down at least twenty minutes. Twenty minutes he couldn't afford.

He wouldn't let the stationary status of the scene he'd been watching for the past five minutes fool him. Everything could change at any moment. Then it would be too late for him to intervene.

For now, all remained the same. The two sentries guarding the only entrance were huddled around a makeshift container where a fire struggled for survival against the merciless desert wind. Three more guard duos surrounded the weather-eaten, sand-brick cabin. From inside the shabby construction, gaslight flickered through the seams of shoddy wooden shutters.

He had to give it to the Aal Ossaibis. The Aal Shalaan's rival clan had constructed a watertight plan, and at the spur of the moment, too. This cabin was in the middle of nowhere. Literally. The nearest inhabited areas were over five hundred miles away in any direction. It was an ideal place to hold a hostage.

The hostage Harres was here to free.

He only found this place because he'd deduced the identity of one of those who hired the people inside the cabin. Since he'd uncovered the plot early enough, he'd managed to tag all the players in transit. He'd followed their phone signals before coverage vanished two hundred miles away. He'd since employed all the technology at his fingertips, and found this place only through some advanced satellite triangulation.

Anyone with less specific knowledge and less-than-limitless access and power at his disposal would have been stymied. Even with all of his resources, he never would have found it if not for his timely deductions.

And time was running out. From what he'd learned of the enemy's plans he had less than twenty minutes to complete the extraction. It was then that the masterminds of this kidnapping would arrive to interrogate the hostage and they'd be bringing their army of guards along.

Under any other circumstances, he wouldn't have considered this the ticking bomb he did now. He would have been here with his own major strike force. The very appearance of his finest Black Ops men would have forced anyone with any survival instincts to throw down his arms in surrender.

But as Zohayd's Minister of Interior and head of Central Intelligence and Homeland Security, he no longer knew whom to trust. His team tonight consisted of three men from his highest-ranking teams whom he would trust with his life. They didn't just work under him—they were family, prince soldiers who, like him, would give their lives for their kingdom. Though in other circumstances he trusted many of his men the same way, he couldn't afford the luxury of belief right now. There was too much at stake, and mixed loyalties could tip the whole region into chaos. He had to treat everyone else as suspect.

How could he not when the royal palace itself had already been breached? He wouldn't put infiltrating his ministry and operations, the forces responsible for keeping Zohayd secure, beyond the royal house's enemies.

He closed his eyes. He could still hardly believe it.

A conspiracy to overthrow his father as king and the Aal Shalaans as the ruling house of Zohayd had been brewing right under their noses for months now. The priceless Pride of Zohayd jewels, believed universally throughout the tribes to give the royal house the right to rule, had been stolen and replaced with fakes just in time for Exhibition Day, when they were to be paraded in public for all to see. No doubt the thief planned to publicly expose the jewels as fakes and begin the chaos that would see the Aal Shalaans removed from power.

For the past weeks, Harres had been casting his net throughout the region using information his brother Shaheen and his new wife, Johara, had secured. Early that morning,

Harres had gotten a lead that might take him straight to the conspiracy's mastermind.

A man claiming to be an American reporter was said to be in possession of all the vital details of the conspiracy.

Within twenty minutes, Harres had arrived at the man's rented condo. But their enemies had already made their move. The man had been gone. Abducted.

Harres hadn't missed a beat since, had followed the trail of the abductors to this desolate place. He had no doubt what the orders of the ruthless patriarch of the Aal Ossaibis were. Extract the info from the man, then let the desert claim him and his secrets.

That alone was reason enough for Harres to be out here. No one would be unjustly hurt on Zohaydan soil on his watch. Not even if it was someone whose agenda was to bring the Aal Shalaans down. Not even if it was this T. J. Burke.

T. J. Burke. The man was an enigma. In his databases Harres possessed up-to-the-moment information on every reporter in the world. He kept tight tabs on each since they wielded the most dangerous weapon of all, the media and its inexorable effect on global movements and the manufacturing of worldwide public opinion.

But T. J. Burke had slipped under his radar. Since Harres had learned of the reporter's existence, the unprecedented had happened. He'd failed to learn anything about the man. It was as if T. J. Burke had come into existence the moment he'd arrived in the region one week ago.

He'd found one reference to the only T. J. Burke who'd ever been in the region, an American IT specialist who'd worked for a multinational corporation in Azmahar. But that man had gone back to the States just over a year ago. A few months later, he'd been tried for the crimes of fraud and embezzlement, perpetrated while he'd been in

Harres's region. He was now serving a five-year sentence in a maximum-security penitentiary and was still securely in his cell as of a couple hours ago.

The current T. J. Burke had probably latched on to the name, or else he'd come up with a random persona for his fictional character and it coincided with an actual person's identity.

Which drove Harres to one conclusion. The man must be a spy. An uncanny one at that, hiding his origins from Harres's networks, and his movements and affiliations, too.

But he would save T. J. Burke even if he were the devil. Once he had him safe, he would extract the info he had. If it was what he hoped, what he feared, he would see what impossible price this man had intended to demand for the invaluable info and double it. Then he'd do everything in his considerable power to ensure he'd never resell it.

The sentries were nodding off in front of the fire now. He signaled to Munsoor, his second-in-command. Munsoor relayed his order counterclockwise to Yazeed at the cabin's south side, who then relayed it to Mohab at its west.

Twice they simultaneously fired their tranq darts, each felling their designated sentries.

Harres erupted to his feet. In seconds he was jumping over the guards' crumpled bodies and landing soundlessly on the stone steps leading to the cabin's door. The others were converging on him.

He exchanged a terse nod with his men, seeing only their intense gazes in the eerie combination of steady-as-time starlight and erratic firelight. They'd deal with any surprises. He'd go straight for their target.

He pushed on the door. It swung open with a creak that gutted the silence.

His gaze swept around the dim interior. Burke wasn't there. There was another room. He had to be there.

He bounded to its skewed door, slowly pushed it open.

A slim, trim-bearded man in a sand-colored quilted jacket rounded on him.

A heartbeat stretched as their eyes clashed.

Even in the faint light, Harres did a double take at the impact of the man's gaze, which seemed to be spewing electric azure. Then there was the rest of him. He seemed to glow in the gloom, both with an incandescent tan and a shock of gleaming gold hair spiking around his face.

Next heartbeat, Harres tore his gaze away, assessed the situation. This was a bathroom. Burke hadn't been using it. He'd been attempting an escape. He'd already pried the six-foot-high window open even with his hands tied in front of him. Harres had no doubt his captors wouldn't have made the mistake of tying them like that. Which meant the man had enough flexibility to get his hands where he could use them. A minute more and he *would* have escaped.

It was clear he didn't know there was nowhere to escape to. He must have been either knocked out cold or blindfolded on the way. But from what he'd seen in Burke's eyes, Harres bet he would have tried to escape regardless. This man was one who'd rather be shot in the back escaping than in the face while he pleaded for his life. He was beyond canny. He was resourceful, fearless.

And he'd be dead if Harres didn't get him out of here.

Harres had no doubt his captors would rather kill the man and lose the info his mind contained than let it fall into Aal Shalaan hands.

Observations segued into action. He lunged, grabbed the man's arm. Next second, he could swear a rocket launched through his teeth and exploded behind his eye sockets. It took him seconds to realize what had happened.

The man had hit him.

Still half-blind, Harres ducked, employing his other senses to dodge the barrage of blows the man rained on him. Harres charged him again, detained him in a crushing bear hug. He had no time for a more intimate introduction to those fists that packed such an unexpected wallop.

The man writhed in his hold with the ferocity of a tornado, almost breaking it.

"Quit struggling, you fool," Harres hissed. "I'm here to save you."

Seemed the man couldn't decipher Harres's words through the shroud covering his mouth. Or he didn't believe him. The man simultaneously delivered a bone-cracking kick to his left shin and kneed him. Harres barely avoided that last crippling impact, marveling at Burke's agility and speed even as he squeezed the man harder. The much smaller, wiry man would give him a run for his money if he had the use of both hands and more space.

Harres wrenched the cloth from his mouth, plastered the man against the uneven stone wall, a forearm against his throat applying enough pressure to make him stop fighting, pushing his face up to his so they again made eye contact.

A buzz zapped through him again as those glowing eyes slammed into his, as the body he imprisoned seethed against his with a mixture of defiance and panic.

Harres shook away the disorientation, firmed his pressure. "Don't make me knock you out and carry you like a sack of dirty laundry. I don't have time for your paranoia. Now, do as I tell you, if you want to get out of here alive."

He didn't wait for the man's consent. But in the second before he wrenched away, he thought he saw the fearful hostility in Burke's eyes soften. He filed away the observation for later dissection as he began dragging Burke back where he'd come from.

A fire exchange ripped the night, aborted his momentum.

Reinforcements must have arrived. His heart stampeded with the need to charge to his men's aid. But he couldn't. They'd all signed on knowing that only securing their target mattered. Anything—and anyone else—was expendable.

Feeling his blood boiling and curdling at once, he turned to the man. They'd have to use the escape route he'd already secured.

The man was ahead of him, already turning there. Harres snatched a dagger from the weapon belt around his thigh, slashed Burke's tethers, put it away, then bent to give him a boost so he could climb out of the window. And the man did another uncanny thing. He leaped up from a standstill, like a cat, clutched the six-foot-high ledge for the moment it took him to gain leverage and impetus to catapult himself through the opening. He cleared it in one fluid move. In a second, Harres heard the distinctive sound of someone hitting the ground on the other side of the wall in a rolling landing.

Was this guy an acrobat? Or was he a Black Ops agent, too?

Whatever he was, he was far more than even Harres had bargained for. He just hoped the tenacious sod didn't take off, forcing him to pursue Burke once he got out of here. It would take him more than the three seconds flat the man had taken to clear that tiny hatch with his size.

In about ten seconds, Harres flipped himself backward through the opening, the only way he'd been able to get enough leverage to squeeze himself through. As he let his mass drag him down, meeting the ground with extended arms, he had an upside-down view of the man's waiting silhouette. So

Burke was intelligent enough to know where his best chances lay.

He landed on flat palms, tucked and flipped over to his feet, standing up and starting to run toward the man in one continuous motion. "Follow me."

Without a word, the man did.

They ran across the sand dunes guided only by Harres's phosphorescent compass and a canopy of cold starlight. He couldn't use a flashlight to find his trail back to his sand car. There was no telling if any of their adversaries had slipped his men's net. A flashlight in this darkness would be like a beacon for the enemy to follow and all this would have been for nothing.

He ran with his charge in his wake, telling himself the others were safe. He wouldn't know for certain until they reached their own helicopter several miles away and entered coverage zones where he could communicate with them.

For now, he could think only of getting T. J. Burke to safety.

Ten minutes later, he felt secure enough to turn his senses back to the man. Burke was keeping up with him. The rhythm of his feet said he was running faster than Harres to make up for the difference in the length of their legs. So not only an agile and ready fighter, but in great shape, too. Good news. He hadn't been looking forward to hauling the guy to the sand car if he collapsed. But it was clear there was no danger of that. Burke was pacing himself superbly. No gasping, just even, deep inhalations and long, full exhalations.

And again something…inexplicable slithered down Harres's body as those sounds seemed to permeate the night, even with his own ears being boxed by the wind. The sensation originated from somewhere behind his breastbone and traveled downward, settling low, then lower.

He gritted his teeth against the disturbance as they reached his sand car. He jumped inside the open-framed, dune-buggy-style four-wheel vehicle. "Get in behind me."

Without missing a beat, Burke slid behind him on the seat, spread his legs on either side of Harres's hips, plastered his front to his back and curled himself around him as if they'd been doing this every day.

A shudder spread through Harres as he revved the motor. In seconds, he was hurtling the sand car over the dunes, driving with even more violence than the urgency of the situation dictated.

He drove in charged silence, catapulting the car over dune edges, crashing it in depressions, spraying sand in their wake and pushing the engine to its limit. With every violent jolt, the man's arms tightened around his midriff, his legs grabbing him more securely, his cheek pressing deeper into his back until Harres felt they'd been fused together.

His breath shortened by the moment as the heat of the man's body seeped through every point of contact, pooled in his loins.

Adrenaline. That was what it was. Discomfort. At having someone pressed so close, even in these circumstances.

Yes. What else could it possibly be?

In minutes, the crouching silhouette of his Mi-17 transport helicopter came into view. It was the best sight Harres had ever seen. He'd not only managed to reach their way out, but now he could get the man off of him.

He screeched the sand car into a huge arc, almost toppling it before bringing it to a quaking stop by the pilot's door.

He wrenched Burke's hands from his waist and leveraged himself out of the car in one motion. The man jumped out behind him, again with the stealth and economy of a cat, then waited for directions.

He took in details now that his vision was at its darkness-adapted best. With his windswept golden hair and those iridescent eyes, Burke looked like some moon elf, ethereal, his beauty untouched by the ordeal—

His *beauty?*

"Jump into the passenger seat and buckle yourself up." He heard his bark, knew all his aggression was directed at his insane thoughts and reactions. "I'll stuff the car in the cargo bay—"

The crack of thunder registered first.

Second, comprehension. A gun's discharge.

The shock in the man's eyes followed.

Last, the sting.

He'd been hit.

Somewhere on his left side, level with his heart. He had to assume not in it. He didn't feel any weakening. Yet.

Someone had slipped his men's net, had managed to sneak up on them. This could be the last mistake he ever made.

He exploded into action, charged the man to stop him from taking cover. They had no time for that.

He shouldn't have worried. Burke was no cowering fool. He was bolting to the helicopter even as more and more gunshots rang around them. He now knew the shot that had connected had been random. That was no sniper out there. That still didn't mean whoever it was couldn't hit a huge target like the chopper.

In seconds they were in their seats and Harres had the monster of a machine roaring off the ground, levitating into the sky.

He pressed the helicopter for all the altitude and velocity it was capable of. In less than a minute he knew they were too far for anyone pursuing them on foot or ATV to even spot anymore.

Only then did he let himself investigate his body for the

damage it had sustained. It had no idea yet. All it reported back was a burning path traversing his left side back to front just below his armpit. Flesh wound, he preferred to assume. Maybe with some bone damage. Nothing major. If no artery had been hit.

But the idea of losing blood too fast and spiraling into shock gave way to more pressing bad news. The chopper was losing fuel. The pursuer had hit the tank.

He eyed the gauge. With the rate of loss, the fuel wouldn't take them back to the capital. Nor anywhere near the inhabited areas where he could make contact with his people.

He had to make a detour. Head for the nearest oasis. At fifty miles away it was still four hundred and fifty miles closer than any other inhabited area. The inhabitants hadn't joined the modern world in any way, but once he and Burke were safely there, he would send envoys on horseback to his people. The trek would probably be delayed by a sandstorm that was expected to cut off the area from the world soon, a week or two during which his brothers and cousins—the only ones who knew of his mission—would probably think him dead. When weighed against his actual survival, and that of his charge, that was a tiny price to pay.

His new plan *would* be effective. Land in the oasis, take care of any injuries and contact his people. Mission accomplished.

Next minute, he almost kicked himself.

Of all times to count his missions….

The leaking fuel wasn't their only problem. In fact it was their slighter one. The damage to the navigation system had taken this long to reveal itself. The chopper was losing altitude fast. And there was nothing he could do to right its course.

He had to land now. Here. Or crash.

He turned to Burke urgently. "Are you buckled in?"

The man nodded frantically, his eyes widening with realization. Harres had no time to reassure him.

For the next few minutes he tried every trick he'd learned from his stint as a test pilot to land the helicopter and not have it be the last thing he did in his life.

As it was, they ended up crash-landing.

After the violent chain reaction of bone-powdering, steel-tearing impacts came to an end, he let out a shuddering breath acknowledging that they had survived being pulverized.

He leaned back in his seat, watching the interior of the cockpit fade in and out of focus. Had he lost too much blood or were the cockpit's lights fluctuating? He had no doubt the chopper itself was a goner.

He'd deal with his own concerns later. After he saw to his passenger.

He unbuckled his belt, flicked the cockpit lights on to maximum, turned to Burke. The man had his head turned against his seat, his eyes wide with an amalgam of panic and relief. Their gazes meshed.

And there was no mistaking what happened then.

Harres hardened. Fully.

He shuddered. What *was* this? What was going on? Was his body going haywire from the stress?

Enough of this idiocy. Check him for injuries.

He reached for him. The man flinched at his touch, as if Harres had electrified him. He knew how he felt. The same charge had forked through him. This had crossed from idiotic to insane.

He forced in an inhalation, determined to erase those anomalous reactions, drew Burke by the shoulders into the overhead light. The man struggled.

"Stop squirming. I need to check you for injuries."

"I'm fine."

The husky voice skewered through him even though he could barely hear it with the din of the still-moving rotors.

And a conviction slammed into him.

He would have thought he was beginning to hallucinate from blood loss. But he'd been feeling these inexplicable things long before he'd been hit. So he was through listening to his mind, and what it thought it knew, and heeding his body. It had been yelling at him from the first moment, just as his every instinct had been. He always listened to them.

Right now they were telling him that, even in these nightmarish conditions, they *wanted* T. J. Burke.

And knowing himself, that could only mean one thing.

He stabbed his fingers into the unruly gold silk on top of T. J. Burke's head, his body hardening more at the escaping gasp that flayed his cheek.

He traced the dewy lips with his thumb, as if to catch the sound and the chagrined shock at what he sensed was an equally uncontrollable response.

He smiled his satisfaction. "So, tell me, why are you pretending to be T. J. Burke, bearded investigative reporter, when a modern-day bejeweled Mata Hari would suit you far better?"

Two

T. J. Burke wrenched away from the cloaked, force-of-nature-in-man-form's hold, panted, voice gruff and low, a tremor of panic traversing it. "Did you hit your head in the crash?"

The man bore down again without seeming to move, making the spacious cockpit of the high-end military helicopter shrink. The smile in those golden eyes that seemed to snare the dimmest rays and emit them magnified, took on a dangerous edge. The danger was more spine-shivering for being unthreatening, more…distressing, with the response it elicited.

Then the colossus drawled in that deeper-than-the-desert-night baritone. "The only hit to the head I got tonight was courtesy of those neatly trimmed, capable hands of yours."

"Since I hit you with the intention of taking your head

off, I probably dislocated something in there. Your good sense, seemingly. Maybe your whole brain."

The man pressed closer, the freshness of his breath and the potency of his virility flooding every one of T.J.'s senses. "Oh, both my sense and my brain are welded in place. It would take maybe…" his eyes traveled up and down T.J.'s body like slow, scorching hands "…ten of you to loosen even my consciousness."

"It took only one of me to do so earlier," T.J. scoffed, not sure the supply of air in the cockpit would last much longer. "I almost took you down. With both hands literally tied, too."

"You can sure take me down, just not by hitting me. Your effect on me has nothing to do with your physical strength and is certainly not proportionate to your size."

"Is that all you got? Cheap shots at my size?"

"I'd never take any kind of shot at you." Again the man's eyes seemed to emit a force field that gathered T.J. into its embrace. "And then, I think your size is perfection itself."

Drenched in goose bumps and feeling the heart that had barely slowed down start to hammer again, T.J. smirked. "Sure you're not concussed? Or is this the way you usually talk to other men?"

The insult seemed to burn to ash in the rising temperature of the man's smile. "It's not even the way I talk to women. But it's the only way I'll talk to *you*. Among other things. Every other possible thing."

T.J. pressed against the passenger door. "So you somehow got it into your head that I'm a woman? And now you're all over me? Just minutes after barely surviving a devastating crash and landing God knows where in this forsaken, sand-infested land? And you can't hear how ridiculous you sound?"

"What's ridiculous is that you thought a fuzzy beard and

an atrocious haircut would disguise the femininity blasting off you. It got me by the…throat, from the first moment. So why don't you drop the act and tell me who you really are?"

"I *am* T. J. Burke!"

Painstakingly chiseled lips spread to reveal teeth so white they were almost phosphorescent in the dimness. "My bearded beauty, only one of us has testosterone coursing in his bloodstream right now. Don't make me offer you… tangible proof."

T.J. glowered at him, tried not to show any weakness, to meet him on the same level of audacity. "Is it the…tangible proof proving that you're attracted to small blond men?"

A chuckle rumbled deep in that huge predator's gut, zigzagged all through T.J.'s system like deadly voltage. "First thing you have to learn about me so we can move on is that I am insult-proof. I wouldn't even sock you if you *were* a man. But my body knew you weren't from the moment I laid eyes on you in that filthy hole, against all evidence and intel. So will you admit it on your own, or will you make me…establish proof myself?"

T.J. shrank back farther against the door as the man's right hand rose. "Lay a hand on me, buster, and have it chomped off."

"With the way I'm reacting to you, there's nothing I want more than your teeth on every part of me. But if anything proves your femininity, it's that so-called threat. A man would have told me he'd break my hand or tear it off, or something suitably macho."

"So you have men regularly threatening to do that? And women chomping away at any part of you they can reach?"

The man narrowed his eyes, concentrating the intensity of his amusement. "You're an expert at diversion, aren't you? Give it up, already. I'm on to you. So on to you that not even a bullet is dulling my response."

"A *bullet?*" T.J felt both eyes almost pop out with shock. "You're hit?"

The man nodded. "So will you take pity on an injured man and bestow your name on me? Make it your real one this time. And let me see how you look without that rug on your face."

"Oh, shut *up*. Are you really injured or are you playing me?"

The man suddenly sat up from his seemingly indolent pose, tugged T.J.'s right hand. T.J. ended up pressed against him, chest to chest, face in his neck, arm around his massive torso. The sensation of touching a live wire came first. Then that of sickening viscosity scorched everything away.

Before T.J. could jerk back in alarm, the man meshed his right hand in T.J.'s hair, pulling gently until their gazes once again melded. "See? I'm bleeding. For you. I might die. Can you be so cruel as to let me die without knowing who you are?"

T.J. wrenched away from him, one hand drenched in the thick heat and slickness of his blood. "Oh, just shut *up*."

Those lethal lips twitched. "I will if you start talking."

"You don't need me to talk, you need me to take care of this wound."

"*I'll* take care of it. You talk."

"Don't be stupid. Your intercostal arteries might be severed, and those bleed like gushing faucets. You might think you're stable, but there's no telling how bad your injury is, what kind of blood loss you've suffered. Your blood pressure could plunge without warning. And if it does, there's no bringing it back up!"

"Spoken like an expert. Been shot before?"

"I've treated people who were. People who weren't too stupid to jump at my offer to help them."

"Is that any way to talk to the man who took a bullet for you? And will you peel that thing off your face, already?"

"I can't believe this! You might slip into shock at any moment and you're still trying to prove this lame theory of yours?"

He just smiled, imperturbable, immovable.

"Okay," T.J. gritted. "I'll talk. After I take care of you."

"I'll let you take care of me. After you talk."

"Come *on*. Where is this chopper's emergency kit?"

"I'll tell you after you tell me what I want to hear."

"Not the truth, huh? 'Cause I already told you that."

The man backed away when T.J. lunged at him, hands reaching out to expose his wound. "Uh-uh-uh. No touching until you admit you're a woman. I only let women touch me."

T.J. glared into eyes that had a dozen devils dancing in them. "You're really out of touch with the reality—the *gravity*—of your situation, aren't you? But what do you care if I admit it or not? You *know* it, after all. And then, I'm not going to merely *touch* you, I'm going to bathe in your blood."

The appreciation in the man's eyes expanded, enveloped T.J. whole. "I knew you were a bloodthirsty wench when you almost sliced me in half with the power of your glare alone. Then you tried to powder my teeth *and* transform me from a baritone to an alto."

T.J. felt a smile advancing, dispelling the frown that by now felt etched on, and had to admit...

That man was lethal. In every sense of the word.

But though he was teasing, his irreversible deterioration

might actually come to pass. There was no telling how serious his injury was without a thorough exam. "And to think you seemed intelligent. Guess appearances can be deceiving."

The man's lips twisted. "You can talk."

"Oh, but I thought my appearance didn't deceive you for a moment, that my 'femininity' kicked you like a mule."

The man sighed, nodding in mock helplessness. "*Aih.* But if I do succumb, remember, it's your doing, in every way."

"Give me a break." T.J. exhaled forcibly then scratched at the beard.

Then she snatched it away.

She yelped as a blowtorch seemed to blast her nerve endings, forcing her to leave the beard dangling over her lips. She rubbed at the burning sensation, gave her tormentor a baleful glance. "Happy now, you pigheaded, mulish ox?"

"A one-man farm, eh? No one has ever flattered me as you do." She glared at him as he oh-so-carefully removed the rest of the beard, making the adhesive separate from her skin with a kneading sensation instead of a stinging one.

Then he pulled back, massaged her jaw and cheeks in an insistent to and fro, soothing her skin with the backs of those long, roughened, steel-hard fingers. She moaned as a far more devastating brand of fire swept her flesh from every point of contact.

He groaned himself. "*Ya Ullah, ma ajmalek.* How absolutely beautiful you are. I thought I'd seen all kinds of beauty, but I've never laid eyes on anything like you. It's like you're made of light and gold and energy and gemstones."

Heat rose through her at his every word. When she'd first seen him, she'd been freezing with dread and the desert's chill. But when she'd turned to him in that filthy bathroom, his very presence had sent animation surging into her every cell. The crash had drained her, but the heat of his solicitude, his awareness and appreciation, the stoking of his challenge, had been melting away the ice that seemed to have become a constituent of her bones.

She still couldn't believe he'd seen through her disguise. No one had during the week she'd been in Zohayd. Her captors hadn't, and she'd spent a whole day in their grasp. But he'd sensed her femininity in moments, with his senses almost blinded by the night's dimness, the urgency and her disguise. He'd also had no tactile evidence, with the buffer of clothes—especially her jacket and the corset flattening her…assets.

Yet he'd known. And just as he'd felt her vibes, she'd been immersed in his. She'd felt every hot granite inch of his formidable body, smelled him over the overpowering stench of her prison, over the dispersion of the desert and the deluge of post-accident mayhem. She'd heard each inflection of his voice through the din of her inner cacophony and the madness of their escape and crash.

And instead of reacting to his maleness as she had to her captors'—with dread, revulsion, aggression and desperation—she was finding it bolstering, soothing and, if she could believe her body's reactions in these insane circumstances, arousing.

She hadn't found a male this arousing in…ever.

And to find this man so might mean it was *she* who'd hit her head. Or something. There must be something wrong, if all she wanted right now was to snuggle into him and hold on tight.

As if responding to her need, mirroring it, he leaned in, pressed his face lightly into her neck, breathed her in and groaned again with intense enjoyment. "Even with male cologne and all the traces of your ordeal, you smell heavenly. And you still haven't told me your name, *ya jameelati.*"

She pulled back from his hypnosis, from the idiocy of her untimely weakness. She had to patch up this obdurate hulk. "And you still think if you ask me enough times I'll give you a different answer."

His eyes stilled on her. Then he nodded, as if coming to a decision. "So your name is T.J. What do the *T* and *J* stand for?"

She blinked. "You believe me?"

"Yes. My instincts about you have been right-on so far. They're saying you're telling the truth now. They even insist you probably haven't developed the ability to lie."

"You make me sound like an incontinent blabbermouth. I gave my kidnappers nothing."

"Withholding the truth is not lying. It can span the spectrum of motives, from fear to nobility. Doing it under threat of harm or worse is courageous. But in almost all situations, telling an untruth is cowardly. And I had no doubt of your courage from the first moment. So, with that established...your name?"

T.J. drew in a shaky inhalation then blurted it out. "Talia Jasmine. Satisfied? Now where is that damned emergency kit?"

She heard his intake of breath, felt it sweeping inside her own chest like an internal caress. But it was the wonder that flared in those preternatural eyes that started her shivering again. With everything but cold.

Without a word, he reached overhead, opened a compartment and produced a huge emergency bag.

She pounced on it. Relief swamped her as she made a lightning-fast inventory of the contents. Everything she could possibly need.

She took out a saline bag, hooked it in an overhead protrusion, dragged his right arm over her lap and pushed the needle into his vein, then secured it with adhesive tape and turned the drip to maximum for quickest fluid replacement.

He tugged at her chin, pressed something to her lips. A bottle of water. She suddenly realized she was beyond parched. She downed the bottle in one go. He watched her as if he wanted to gulp her down himself, to decipher and assimilate her.

She licked her lips, cleared her throat. "Okay, I need you to expose the wound and hold this flashlight over it for me. Better do it in the back of this monster so you can lie down."

He smiled in that seriousness-melting way of his. "I can give you two out of three of your demands. I can with pleasure take off my clothes. And I can shed light on the mess I made when all of my senses were so focused on you that I missed the pursuer who could have killed me with one haphazard shot. I shudder to think where that would have left you."

"As if I'm in such a great situation now," she mumbled under her breath as she snapped on gloves.

"We're both in one piece, with me only slightly punctured, which in a hostage-extraction op is about the best possible situation. But I have to inform you I had to sacrifice the back end of the chopper to preserve the cockpit while crash-landing. I doubt there's any space back there for even one of *your* species to stretch out."

She looked up from preparing her surgical tray. "My species? Women you mean? Last I heard we were a gender."

"Felines." His smile widened as he reached for the swathe over his head to start the process of exposing himself…his *wound* for her. "I know of nothing else capable of exiting a six-foot-high window with as much economy of movement and grace."

"They're called gymnasts. I was one till I hit eighteen. Seems my abilities reactivated under duress."

He finished unfurling the yards of material from his head in movements she could only describe as...erotic. This was a man used to barricading himself in mere cloth before plunging into the desert, pitting his wiles and will against its cruelty and capriciousness.

Suddenly all thoughts evaporated. The last coil fell off, and a mane of gleaming mahogany cascaded in layers of satin luxury to his shoulders.

She swallowed. "You should talk."

"Oh?" One formidable wing of an eyebrow quirked as he shrugged off the outer layer of his night-colored desert raider/ninja/Black Ops hybrid outfit. He seemed to grow bigger in only a skintight, high-collared, long-sleeved top.

She gave him an encompassing gesture. "You should be on stage playing the Lion King yourself. With minimal or no makeup."

And he gifted her with another of those amused rumbles that proved his great feline origins.

Then he tried to yank off his top and groaned, his face twisting in obvious pain. "Seems raising my left arm won't be one of my favorite activities for a while."

"Do you have a change of clothes on board?"

"Yes. And other supplies that I'll access once we're done with this."

"Okay, then." She swept scissors off the tray and proceeded to cut off his top.

He hissed as the coolness of the blade slid against his hot skin, groaned as she reached the parts that had stuck to his wound, then growled as her gloved hands glided over his flesh, separating the adhesions and palpating the edges of his wound.

There should only be pain. But to ears that were hyperaware of his merest inflection, the pleasure was unmistakable, too.

Tremors invaded her hands, traveling all the way from her core. And this from gloved and accidental contact while exploring his wound. What would touching him with no barriers do to her if she were exploring his power and beauty for pleasure instead?

Work, idiot. Stop fantasizing about this hunk of impossible virility and just patch him up. You're probably in ten different types of shock and hallucinating most of this anyway. Moron.

Continuing her raucous inner abuse, she worked in silence.

Suddenly a realization dawned on her. All the time she'd been filling hypodermic needles with local anesthetic, analgesic/anti-inflammatory and broad-spectrum antibiotic, he'd been handing her vials, receiving filled syringes and placing them in the correct sequence on the tray like the best of her long-term assistants. He continued to help her with total efficiency and obvious knowledge of what went where and would be used when as she prepared forceps, scalpels, sutures, cautery, bandages, wipes and antiseptics.

He hadn't been bragging when he'd said he'd take care of his wound. This was a man versed in more than hostage-retrieval ops. He was no stranger to field emergency procedures.

Just who and what was he?

She opened her mouth to ask and one of those fingers she'd bet could bend steel feathered down her cheek again. The gentleness of his touch almost pulverized her precarious control. Tears churned at the back of her eyes. She swallowed them along with any questions.

He asked them of her. "You weren't exaggerating when you said you'd treated bullet wounds before. Just who are you, my heaven's dew?"

Her hands stilled from checking her supplies before she started the procedure.

No one had ever realized the meaning of her name.

"Your parents are to be applauded for choosing such a name to befit your wonder and delicacy."

She shot him an affronted look. "I'm not delicate!"

His smile filled with teasing indulgence. "Oh, but you are, incredibly so."

She narrowed her eyes at him. "How's your jaw?"

Something hot and delighted rumbled deep in his chest, revved in her bones like a bass line made of urges instead of sound. "My jaw will always remember its meeting with your fist. But sheathe your claws. Delicacy doesn't equate with fragility when describing you, but with refinement mixed with delectability wrapped around a core of resourcefulness. That's what you are. An exterior of pure gold, a filling of sheer delight and a center of polished steel."

Her lips twitched. "You sure you didn't hit your head? Or are you always so ready and free with spontaneous poetry?"

"I'm the very opposite. Women call me a miser with words. I never say what I don't mean. What I don't feel. It's no wonder I was chosen for law enforcement and not diplomacy."

"So among the hordes of women who've stampeded through your life, I'm the only one who, in the aftermath of a rescue mission out of a *Mission Impossible* movie, has moved you so much you've found your inner poet."

"You've summed it up perfectly."

He suddenly turned around and lay back, placing his head and shoulders on her lap.

He grinned up at her as she froze, stared down at him. "This is the only place I'm lying down around here."

She gulped, looked into his upside-down eyes and repressed the urge to smooth her hands over his face, to thread her fingers through that incredible mane fanned over her lap, and most insane of all, to bend down and kiss his forehead before she started poking him with needles and slicing him with scalpels.

Before she succumbed to any of those ridiculous urges, he transferred the tray she'd prepared to the floor, then turned to his side to present her with an optimum view of his injury.

She almost choked when he looked up from his sideways position and purred, "And that's the best way to hand you instruments as you work."

She gave a jerky nod and a throat-clearing cough, hoping to expel any mind-fogging stupidity.

Then proceeded to examine his wound.

Harres looked up at this enigma in a woman's form whom he'd saved. And who was in turn saving him.

He held the flashlight at an optimal angle for her. And while she injected his side with local anesthetic, he examined her.

She was beyond beautiful. Unique. Magical. He hadn't told her the half of it when she'd charged him with being poetic.

She finally made that throat-clearing noise he'd come to realize meant she was fighting for composure. And he bet it had nothing to do with the medical part of their situation.

"Okay. The bullet made a clear track through your muscles. It hit the tip of your scapula, grazing three ribs.

No tendons or nerves are severed. There is muscle damage at the bullet's entry point, then as it came out the front it tore a four-inch wound in your skin. But the bleeding is the worst of it, since a few arteries have recoiled out of reach. I'll have to widen the wound and deepen it, to fish them out and cauterize them, and for future drainage. I'll place deep sutures to repair the most traumatized tissues, but will leave the wound open to drain for later closure, once the swelling goes down, so no infection is trapped within."

As she spoke, she continued to implement her plan with flawless execution. He continued to assist her.

Every minute brought more unprecedented sensations. It wasn't just physical reactions to feeling her firm, warm thighs beneath his head, or breathing her hot, intoxicating scent with every breath. He'd never experienced this synergy, not even when working with his brothers or his men. He'd never let another person take charge of anything while he was around, let alone his own physical well-being. He'd never lusted after a woman anywhere near this intensely, let alone while simultaneously respecting the hell out of her capabilities, relying on her efficiency and wanting to pamper her with all he had and protect her with his life.

Was this real, or was everything being amplified by the circumstances combined with a dose of blood loss, survival elation and gratitude?

But when he added in his mounting physical response and mental appreciation, he was back to square one.

This *was* as real as anything got. And from the way she kept stroking him with her eyes after she finished each step and with her hands after each cut as if to apologize for the necessity of hurting him to heal him, from the way her hands and lips trembled at his merest indication of discomfort, he knew.

It was just as real for her.

It didn't matter who they were, or how and when they'd met. What they'd done since, the seeming lifetime of life-changing events and feelings they'd experienced together, meant they could leap over most stages of development and acknowledgment of attraction.

She finished the procedure and he sat up, helped her wrap his torso in bandages. As she began to draw back, he couldn't bear it. His right hand wove into her hair, kept her close, brought her closer. And she lurched away.

He stilled, his heart jolting with the same force.

After a long moment, he removed his hand, whispered, "Are you afraid of me?"

"No." Relief deflated him at her vehement denial. Then she grinned sheepishly at him, boosting her beauty to dizzying heights. "Which might be the stupidest thing I've ever thought or felt, considering I'm in the middle of nowhere with a hulk of a man in a hostile land where I know no one. But there you go. I'm not afraid of you. Not for a second. I'm…the very opposite."

Warmth flooded him at her admission. He'd been right. She felt the same way.

Another unknown urge took him over, the desire to tease her, even as he wanted to devour her. "Now that's a little white lie. You were so afraid of me for at least a few seconds that you almost gave me a permanent disability."

"That was before I saw your face, heard your voice. Before that, you were this…huge chunk of night that had come to claim me."

"You were right about the coming to claim you part." He reached out to her again, slid a hand around her waist, drew her to him. "So are you going to tell me where you learned to perform field surgery like that?"

"In medical school, where else?"

"You mean you *are* a doctor?"

"Last I heard that's what came off said school's production line."

"So everything I thought you were was false, from your gender to your profession. Is there no end to your surprises?"

A grin trembled on her dimpled but now colorless lips. "Now why would there be?"

The urge to capture her lips, nibble color and warmth back into them surged inside him, almost brimmed over into action.

"No reason at all, *ya shafeyati*."

"What does this mean?"

"My healer."

"So how do you say 'my rescuer' in Arabic?"

"Monqethi."

She repeated the word after him, that voice that even when she'd tried to deepen and roughen it had coursed through him like an intravenous aphrodisiac now becoming a vocal caress that soothed his insides, infused his every cell.

Then she heightened her exquisite torture. "And 'my hero'?"

His vocal cords locked against the tide of temptation. He whispered, *"Buttuli,"* listened to her hypnotic melody begin to repeat it, before his control snapped.

He swooped down and took the rest of her tremulous homage inside him, along with that breath that had been tormenting him with its arousing fragrance. She gave him more, in one gasp after another, opened for him.

He wanted to drown in her, drown her in him, give her a glimpse of the need and ferocity she ignited in him. His lips claimed hers as if he'd brand her, his tongue thrusting deep, breaching her, draining her of moans and sweetness.

She took it all, seeming unable to meet his passion yet overwhelming him with her surrender.

"Talia…*nadda jannati*…my heaven's dew…"

"Not fair," she moaned into his lips. "I don't know your name…let alone what it means."

He drew in her plump lower lip, suckled it until she cried out and took his tongue deeper.

"Harres…Harres Aal Shalaan." He started to translate, had said only "Guardian—" when she gasped then pushed him away.

He stared down at her, all his being rioting, needing her back against him, her lips crushed beneath his, her heat enveloping his suddenly chilled body.

She gaped up at him.

Then she finally rasped, "You're an Aal Shalaan?"

Harres nodded, already acutely sorry that he'd told her.

Now it would end, the spontaneity of the attraction that had exploded to life between them. Now that he'd told her who he was, nothing could ever be the same. There hadn't been a woman of the thousands he'd met in his life, the hundreds who'd pursued him, no matter how attracted to him they were, who'd seen him as anything but an amalgam of status, power and money. He was never just a man to them. He'd cease to be just a man to her now.

He exhaled, his gaze leaving her kiss-swollen lips in regret as he waited for artificiality to settle into her guileless eyes, for calculation to take hold of her open-book reactions. He'd often chafed at the trappings of his status and position and wealth. He now positively cursed them.

Then she again did the last thing he could have expected.

Her gaping became a glare of such revulsion and hostility,

he might as well have turned into a slimy creature before her eyes.

Then she spat, "You're one of that pack of highborn, lowlife criminals?"

Three

Harres stared at this woman who'd just called him and his family a pack of criminals. And he did the only thing he could.

He threw his head back and belted out a guffaw.

Now that the local anesthetic was wearing off, his wound protested the uninhibited movement, stabbed him with a burning lance of pain. It wasn't any hotter than the glare of abhorrence Talia still scorched him with. Seemed his mirth only poured fuel on her sudden antipathy.

But he couldn't help it. There was no way he could control his relief, his thrill, that instead of fawning over him, she looked ready to sock him again.

Then she did. On his good arm, hard enough to sober him a bit, save him from tearing loose her meticulous suturing efforts with laughter.

"Don't you laugh at me, you aggravating jackass!"

As if in response to her anger, the wind exploded with sudden fury around the helicopter, rocking the wreckage.

She didn't seem to notice as she braced herself, her incandescent eyes riddling him with azure-hot holes.

And he just loved it.

He raised a placating hand, tried to pretend a measure of sobriety. It was far harder than anything he'd done tonight. Right along with not reaching out and dragging her back against him. The woman sabotaged his propriety sense and either caressed, aroused or tickled all others.

"I wouldn't dare. And then, this is delight, not ridicule." His left hand rubbed the sting of her blow, as if to trap the feel of her flesh against his, even in anger. His lips were still burning with the memory of capturing hers, his tongue from tangling with hers, tasting her intoxication and swallowing her whimpers of pleasure. All of him still tingled from having her, ton of clothes and all, pressed against him. He wanted to get this confrontation out of the way so he could have her there again. "And it's your doing again, you and your endless surprises."

She balled her fists, her bee-stung lips pressing into an ominous line. "How about I give those a fitting end? By fracturing your nose."

Her aggression made the pleasure bubbling inside him spill again into a chuckle as he gave his aching jaw a reminiscent rub. "To go with my jaw?" He turned his face, presented her with a three-quarters view of said nose. "Or do you think it could do with a new one?" He shook his head at her chagrined hiss. "Whoa, that alone could have done the job. It's a good thing I didn't tell you my name when you had your scalpels deep in my flesh."

Her eyes became slits of enraged challenge. "But now I know it, and I'll have those scalpels there again while debriding the wound before closing it. Over many stages.

Or it will fester. And don't tell me you can take care of it yourself, 'cause we both know you can't. Most of the wound track is where you can't reach it. And next time, maybe my nerve block won't be as…effective."

He gasped in mock shock. "You not only flaunt your power over me, you'd abuse that power, disregard your oath to do no harm? You would torment me while I'm under your scalpel? You'd gloat at my helplessness and need, and take pleasure in my pain?" He let excitement at her implied threat spread his lips. "I can't wait."

Her eyes swept him with now blue-cold disdain. "So you have an extreme form of masochism among your perversions, huh? Figures."

"Not to me, it doesn't. At least, it didn't. But I *am* discovering I'd welcome anything from you."

She snorted. He shook his head as he huffed another chuckle. He couldn't believe it himself, how fully he meant that.

Sighing, admitting that for the first time in his life, he was experiencing something beyond his control, he reached for what had survived of his bloody clothes. And though she aimed more detestation at him, he felt her unwilling coveting spread over every inch of his cold flesh, heating it from the inside out. He shuddered at the caress of her eyes over every bulge and stretch of his muscles as he carefully pulled his clothes back on.

His satisfaction rose. Her reactions to him had not only alternated between delightful and brutal honesty, they were as overpowering as his. Her mind might be telling her to slash him open, but everything else was clamoring for his nearness, delighting in his every detail. And of course that was making her madder. At him.

He'd finished dressing before it occurred to him to try the heater. It was still working.

He turned his gaze back to her with a smile, and she slammed him with a disapproving scowl.

"*Now* you turn on the heater. Were you trying to see how long you can last before you succumb to hypothermia? Or were you hoping I'd offer you the best remedy for it?"

"Flesh-on-flesh warming." He almost shivered with imagining the mind-melting sensuality of such an act with her. "And now you've cornered me. I must admit either that I was such a remiss male that I didn't think of it, or such an inefficient field officer that I didn't remember the onboard heater. Will I get leniency points if I cite my reason for failing to think of it to be preoccupation with your golden self?"

"Nah. I have another explanation. You didn't think of it because you're cold-blooded like all *your* species. Snakes."

A laugh overpowered him and sent another bolt of pain through him. "Ah, I've never been so inventively insulted before. I can't get enough of whatever spills from your mouth."

Her smile was one of condescension and disgust. "I'm such a refreshing acid bath after all the slimy, simpering sweetness you usually marinate in, huh, you jaded jerk?"

He put a protective hand to his side as he laughed again and groaned in pain simultaneously. "What you are is literally sidesplitting. It is positively intoxicating what an irreverent, fearless wildcat you are, *ya nadda jannati*."

"Don't you dare call me that again!" she growled.

"Talia…"

She slammed her fist on her thigh in chagrin. "And don't call me that, either. I'm T.J.—no, *Dr.* Burke to you. No—I'm nothing to you. So don't call me anything at all!" He began to say her name again but she bulldozed over his insistence. "And now I take back everything *I* called you.

You're not *monqethi* or *buttuli*. You're just one of those self-serving, criminal dictators. Or wait—since you were sent to retrieve me, you're probably one of their lower ranks, maybe even disposable. Not that it makes you any better than the higher-ups."

Everything inside him stilled.

Then he slowly asked, "You don't know who I am?"

"You're an Aal Shalaan," she spat the name. "That's all I need to know."

Would knowing exactly who he was change her attitude? For the better? By now, he was hoping it would. Her antagonism, now that it seemed there to stay, was fast losing its exciting edge.

Then he inhaled. "I'm not just an Aal Shalaan. I'm Harres."

"Yeah, I heard you the first time. But just Harres, huh? Like you're Elvis or something!"

"Around here? I'd say I'm more Captain Kirk. And you really have no idea, eh?"

Her eyes narrowed on him. "So you're some big shot?"

He huffed, the last traces of elation snuffed. "The third-biggest shot around, yes."

He saw that lightning-fast mind of hers reach the conclusion. She still stared at him, as if expecting him to say something else to negate his declaration and her deduction.

He quirked a prodding eyebrow at her. He wanted to reach the new status quo his identity always triggered and be done with it.

She shook her golden head dazedly, her lips opening and closing on many aborted outbursts, before she finally managed to voice one.

"You're *that* Harres Aal Shalaan?"

"You mean there are others? And here I thought I was the one and only."

"And here I thought the dumb-blonde stereotype had been long erased. Clearly not in Zohayd, if you think I'll believe *that*."

"Actually I think you're superiorly intelligent and extensively informed. In general. In this specific case, I think you're suffering from severe and very damaging misinformation."

"Fine. One of the hallmarks of superior intelligence is an open mind. So here's my mind, wide as the desert and ready for amending info. What is the king's second son and Zohayd's worshipped minister of interior doing on a hostage-retrieval mission?"

"You see? Brilliant. You cut to the core of logic in any situation like an arrow. And as the question is the only one to be asked, the answer is as singular. I couldn't entrust anyone else with retrieving you. I had to be here myself. And I thank the circumstances that necessitated my presence."

She cracked a bitter laugh. "Sure, because it turned out to be me, and I'm unique, magical, and our meeting under these circumstances is an unprecedented and unrepeatable act of munificent fate, and all that over-the-top drivel."

His hands itched with the need to capture that proud, obstinate head, subdue her resentment, resurrect her hunger.

But he knew that would backfire. He was finally realizing the gravity of the situation. The depth of her prejudice. He had no idea what had formed such an iceberg within her, but if he wasn't careful, all his efforts to win her trust would be wrecked against it.

He let the last trace of the smile go. This needed to be serious, heartfelt. That would be easy. He didn't have to act either sentiment. "A few minutes ago, before learning my identity turned you from an ally into an enemy, you would have agreed with all that you now consider devious nonsense."

Her eyes lashed him with more vexation. He realized that her belief that she'd been taken in was exaggerating her anger. "Sure I would have. I was being worked by a master manipulator. But then, after I escaped being interrogated to death by a gang of desert hooligans, anyone would have seemed a knight in camouflage to my fried mind and senses. But you're not being very clever. Telling me who you are was the worst mistake you could have made. You would have served your goal far better if you'd let me believe you were small fry, one of the hundreds of 'princes' with the odd drop of Aal Shalaan blood. Exposing yourself as the premium pure brew only makes you more accountable for the crimes your family perpetrated. It makes you the enemy I'm here to bring down."

Talia watched her words sink into Harres Aal Shalaan.

She'd managed to wipe away that indulgent smile that had seemed permanent on his face a couple of minutes ago. Now she'd gone a dozen steps further, causing his expression to be engulfed in a tide of grimness.

She almost bit her tongue, but she might get poisoned by the venom flowing from it.

But she couldn't stop. Disappointment urged her to pour it out before it ate through her. Her hero, her savior, the man who'd risked his life to rescue her, was an Aal Shalaan. And not just any Aal Shalaan. One of the four big guns. And the one who had as much jurisdiction and even more law-enforcement power than the king himself. Which meant only one thing.

He had more to lose than any other member of his family.

He had *everything* to lose.

And she was using her considerable provocation powers to declare herself in a position to affect those incalculable losses. While she was stranded in the desert with him, with no way of rejoining humanity except through him.

Any bets she ever would now?

She held her breath for his reaction. So rage and indignation and—damn him—*him* were loosening every last one of her discretion screws. But not to the point where she'd lost track of the possible, and expected, consequences.

He lowered his gaze, relinquishing hers for the first time. She watched the long sweep of his downcast lashes as they stilled, her heart ramming her ribcage. Next time he raised those eyes he'd take off the mask of geniality and tolerance. They'd be cold and ruthless. And he'd no longer be her persuader but her interrogator, not her rescuer but her warden.

Then he raised his eyes and almost had her keeling over in his lap.

Those golden orbs were emitting a steady energy, a calming power that seeped through hers, into her brain, flooding her whole body.

The son of a…king was trying to hypnotize her!

And he was almost succeeding. Even now.

So. She'd gravely underestimated him. She'd thought, with the novelty of her resistance depleted, his facade of endless patience and indulgence would crack, exposing his true face. That of an all-powerful prince used to having people cower before him. But it seemed he was also an infallible character-reader, realized that intimidation would get him nowhere with her. So he wasn't playing that card just yet. Not before he gave all the others in his formidable arsenal a full demo.

So Prince Harres Aal Shalaan wasn't who he was just

because he'd been delivered into the royal family, hadn't qualified for his position in the family business because he'd grown up playing desert raiders. He evidently had staying power, was in command of himself at all times. He had long-term insight and layered intelligence, remained on top of any situation. And he had uncanny people skills and truckloads of charisma, made willing followers of everyone he crossed paths with.

He had of her, too. But no more.

The bucket of drool stopped here.

Then he spoke in that polyphonic voice of his, which made her feel as if it was coming from all around her, from inside her, and she almost revised her certainty. Almost.

"I don't know what you've been hearing about the Aal Shalaans, or from whom, but you've been misled. We're neither despots nor criminals."

"Sure. And I'm supposed to take your word for it."

"Yes, until I'm in a position to prove it. I would at least demand you grant us the benefit of the doubt."

"Oh, if I had any, I'd grant it. But I don't, so I won't."

"Won't you at least make your accusations and give me a chance to come up with a defense?"

"I'm sure you can come up with anything you wish. You'd fabricate enough evidence to confuse issues with reasonable doubt. But this isn't a court of law, and I'm not a judge. I'm just someone who knows the truth. And I'm here collecting evidence to prove it."

"To prove what?"

"That you're not all above reproach as you paint yourselves to be."

He gave a shrug with his right shoulder. It was eloquent with concession and dismissal. The man spoke, expressed, with every last inch of his body. "Who in any place of power doesn't have someone with a beef against them?

Ruling a country isn't all plain sailing. Laws and rulings are contested, whether economic, military or judicial, by others with opposing views or interests. In my own peacekeeping and business capacities, I'm sure my decisions and actions always leave someone disgruntled. That doesn't mean I'm evil. I've certainly done nothing criminal in my life."

"Oh, you're too clever to do something overt. But you, Mr. Peacekeeping Entrepreneur, manipulate the law, and people. Like you did me. Like you're still trying to. But I'm on to you. I'm on to your whole family. That you call yourselves a royal family doesn't make you any less criminal. Many so-called rulers were deposed then brought to justice for crimes against their people. As you one day, and soon I hope, will be."

Okay. She'd done it. She'd ensured her place at the top of his blacklist.

And again, the tenacious man refused to get it over with and validate her fear, release his mask.

His face remained the very sight of sincerity, his voice the very sound of earnestness. "You can believe what you wish, Talia. But I will also say what I wish, my version of the truth. I would have come to save you, no matter who you were. And whomever I saved would have been safe with me. Whatever your agenda is, you are safer with me than with your own family. You scoff now, but when you weren't applying your prejudice to me, you, too, believed it was an act of fate for us to share this, to feel this powerfully about each other, to see the other for what we truly are without the help or hindrance of identities and history. I now urge you to look beyond what you think you know, to what you *do* know. Of me. You're a doctor, and you're used to seeing people stripped to their basic nature during emergencies. You've seen me as I really am through the best tests of all—the litmus of mortal danger, and your own valiant efforts at exercising your potent provocation."

She gaped at him for a long moment.

Then she shook her head on a bewildered, belligerent chuckle. "You *should* have been a diplomat. You'd hog-tie anyone in a net of platitudes and persuasions so thick, they wouldn't see the way out and would soon stop wanting one. But it's too late with me, so save it."

His gaze lengthened in turn. She could swear he was struggling not to smile again. At last he exhaled, like a man bound on tolerating a nuisance for life, leveled that supernatural gaze on her. "You believe you have reason to hate us. Tell me."

"I'm telling you nothing. As far as I'm concerned, you're no better than my kidnappers. You're actually far worse. My enmity with them was incidental. I was just the source of damaging info to their hereditary enemies. But with your family, my enmity is very specific. And don't play the 'I took a bullet saving you' card. I now realize why you did. You want what they wanted. And my answer to you is the same one I gave them. You can go take a flying leap from one of your capital's world-record-high skyscrapers."

"Is that how you always reach your verdicts, Talia? You judge by symptoms that have many differential diagnoses and insist on the first one that occurs to you and explains them?"

She gritted her teeth against the urge to punch him again. The man made perfect sense every time he opened his mouth. Was there no provoking him into making his first mistake? "Oh, don't start with the professional similes. You know nothing about me."

"I may not know the facts about you, but I know a lot about the truth. I'm certain of everything I know, through the proof of your actions in the worst possible conditions.

You're brave and daring and capable and intense. You're passionate in everything you do and about everything you believe in, most of all your sense of justice. Be fair with me now. Give me a chance to defend my family. Myself. Please, Talia, tell me."

His every word expanded in her heart like a compulsion trying to spread out and take hold of her. She resisted his influence, slammed him with her frustration. "I told you not to call me that. But since you're breath-depleting and you can talk me under the sand, just call me T.J. if you must call me at all. Everyone does."

This time he let that smile spread on his lips again. "Then something's wrong with everyone you know, if they can look on your beauty and think something as sexless and characterless as T.J., let alone articulate it. I'm calling you nothing but Talia. Or *nadda jannati*. It's impossible for me not to. Deal with it."

She gave a smothered screech. "For Pete's sake, turn off your female-enthrallment software. It won't work anymore. It's making me so sick that I'd rather you use your fists like my captors did."

It was as if she'd hit a button, fast-forwarding his face from teasing to ominous. He rasped, "They hit you?"

She instinctively rubbed the lingering ache in her gut, which had been swamped by far more pressing urgencies. "Oh, a couple did, just for laughs. It wasn't part of the interrogation, since those jerks weren't cleared to engage in that, and I bet their orders were not to damage me. But they couldn't resist bullying the smaller man they thought I was. One made it sound as if it's some duty a true Zohaydan owes any foreigner messing in the kingdom's business."

His teeth made a bone-scraping sound. "I wish I had used something other than tranq darts to knock them out. Something that would have caused permanent damage"

She gave an impressive snort. "Stop pretending to care."

"I can't stop something I'm not pretending. And I would have cared had you been a man, even the spy with the multiple agenda I thought you to be. Nothing is more despicable or worthy of punishment than abusing the helpless. Under any pretext. Those men aren't patriots as they pretended, they're vicious, cowardly lowlifes who can't pass up a chance to take their deficiencies out on those who can't retaliate."

"Right. Like you're the defender of the weak and the champion of the oppressed."

He gave a solemn nod. Then, as if he was renewing a blood oath, he said, "I am."

And she couldn't hold back, blurted it all out. "Like you defended my brother? Like you championed him against the bullies in your family who abused their power and threw him in jail?"

Four

Harres had thought he'd been ready for anything.

He had made peace with the fact that he would never know what to expect next from Talia Jasmine Burke.

But this was beyond unexpected. And he wasn't ready for it.

He stared into her eyes. They were flaying him with rage. But now anxiety muddied their luminous depths. It fit what he knew of her, that his first sighting of the debilitating emotion there wouldn't be on her own account, but on a loved one's.

Her brother.

So that was it. Why she was here.

He knew she'd been determined not to tell him, hated that she had, was madder than ever, at herself. But it was out.

At least, the first clue was. He realized she was talking

about the same T. J. Burke he'd investigated. There couldn't be another one who happened to be in jail, too.

That still didn't tell him why she'd implicated his family in her brother's imprisonment. And it was clear he had another fight on his hands until she gave him anything more.

After a long moment of refusing to give an inch, her whole body started shaking from escalating tension, her eyes growing brighter as pain welled in them. His insides itched with the need to defuse her agitation. But he was the enemy to her now. She wouldn't let him console her while she considered him—however indirectly—the cause of her brother's suffering.

Struggling not to override her resistance and to hell with the consequences, maybe even letting her vent her surplus of anguish by lashing out at him, he let out a ragged exhalation. "You've come this far. Tell me the rest."

She glared defiance at him then echoed his exhalation. "Why? So you can tell me I got it all wrong again? You've said that a few times already. I'll cut and paste on my own."

"*Oqssem b'Ellahi,* I swear to God, Talia, if you don't start talking, I'll kiss you again."

Outrage flared in her eyes. And, he was certain, unwilling remembrance and involuntary temptation, too. That only seemed to pour fuel on her indignation. He would have been thrilled that her attraction was so fierce it defied even her hostility. *If* the grimness of the situation wasn't mounting by the second. Then she thrilled him anyway.

She hissed, "My earlier 'feminine' threat of chomping a part of you off stands. It'll just be your lips instead of your hand."

He inclined his head at her, suppressing the smile spreading inside him. He couldn't exhibit any levity. She'd only put the worst possible interpretation to it. "Why bother when you'd only end up fixing it? Talk, Talia. If I'm to be punished for it, at least face me with the details of my charge."

Her scowl darkened. "I again remind you I'm not the police. I don't owe you a reading of the charges against you. I'm the family of the victim, and you're the family of the criminals."

"So what did my family of criminals do?" he prodded. "Don't leave me in suspense any longer."

She huffed some curses about his being a persistent pain in the posterior under her breath, then finally said, "My brother—my *twin*—" she paused to skewer him with a glare of pure loathing "—was working in Azmahar two years ago. He's an IT whiz, and international companies have been stealing him from each other since he turned eighteen. He met a woman and they fell in love. He asked her to marry him and she agreed. But her family didn't."

So a woman was involved. Figured. Not that he'd expected it.

"The woman's name is Ghada Aal Maleki." She watched him as she pronounced the foreign-to-her name in perfect precision, eyes probing, shrewd. Then she smirked. "Do turn down the volume of the bells ringing in your head. Very jarring now that the desert seems to have turned in for the night."

He contemplated the implications of the new information even as his lips twitched at her latest bit of lambasting. "Excuse the racket. Bells did go off quite loudly. The woman in question belongs to the royal family of Azmahar. I know she's long been betrothed. But what caused the jangling is to whom. Mohab Aal Shalaan, my second cousin and one of the three men on my retrieval team tonight."

Her mouth dropped open. Then she threw her hands

in the air, looked around as if seeking support from an invisible audience as she protested the unfairness of this last revelation. "Oh, great. Just super dandy. So now I'm supposed to owe *him* my life, too?"

He shook his head, adamant. "You don't owe anyone anything. We were doing our duty. As for Mohab and Ghada's betrothal, it was family-arranged, but I have a feeling both have been working together to sabotage their families' intentions. She first insisted on obtaining her bachelor's degree, then she wanted to finish her postgraduate studies and he gladly agreed, granting her year after year of postponement. I think both want to escape marriage altogether and are using each other as an alibi for as long as they can put off their families. As of hours ago, there's been no sign of a wedding date being set."

She digested this then raised her chin, trying to seem uninterested. "Well, maybe your second cousin doesn't want to marry Ghada, but your family wants him to, at any cost. Must have some huge vested interest in the marriage so they'll do anything to see it comes to pass. When Ghada told them she was breaking it off with your cousin and marrying my brother, they drove him away from Azmahar. But when Ghada said she'd join him in the States, they decided to get rid of him altogether.

"They fabricated a detailed hacking-and-embezzlement history implicating him in major cyber raids. They somehow got the States to arraign him and put him on trial. He was found guilty in less than two months and sentenced to five years. After the first couple of weeks there, they even arranged for him to be attacked. When he defended himself, he became ineligible for good behavior. So now he'll serve the full sentence without possibility of parole. In a maximum-security prison."

Silence detonated after the last tear-clogged syllable

tumbled from her lips. Only the harsh unevenness of her breathing broke the expanding stillness as her eyes brimmed then overflowed with resurrected anguish, outrage and futility.

And she was waiting for him to make a comment. He had none.

She on the other hand, had plenty more. "T.J.—yeah, that's his name, too, Todd Jonas—looks like me, Prince Harres. I'm tall for a woman, but imagine a five-foot-eight man who doesn't have much on me in breadth and who's got my coloring and the eternally boyish version of my features. Do you have any idea what prison is like for him? I die each day thinking what his life is like on the inside. He's got four years and seven months more to serve. All thanks to your family."

He could only stare at her. He knew in gruesome detail what she was talking about. A prison full of the lowlifes he'd just described, preying on the weakest of the herd. With her brother as an easy, eye-catching target.

She went on, a fusion of terrible emotions vibrating in her voice. "But no thanks to all of you, he's safe. For now. I…buy his safety. I probably won't be able to afford it for long, as the premium keeps going up. In the past three months it has already tripled."

This time when she fell silent, he knew she'd said all she was going to say.

It was endless minutes before he could bring himself to talk. "Nothing I say could express my regret at your brother's situation. If it's true any member of my family was responsible—"

"If?" Her sharp interjection cut him off. "Oh, it is true, Prince Harres. And I've been given the chance to prove it. And to do something about it."

He couldn't help coming closer with the urgency her fiery

conviction sparked in him. "What exactly? And given? By whom?"

She looked at him as if he'd told her to jump out of a plane without a parachute and he'd catch her. "As if I'd tell you."

"It's vital that you tell me, Talia," he persisted. "If I know all the details, I can help. I will."

"Sure you will. You'll help prove your own family guilty of fraud, send those involved to jail instead of my brother."

"I can't say what will happen, since I don't know the specifics, but if there's anything I can do to help your brother, I will do it."

She smirked at him. "*That's* more like it. Be inconclusive, make insubstantial promises. Until the silly goose gives you what you bothered to come after her for."

He leveled his gaze on her, tried to convey all the sincerity he harbored in this specific situation and the rules he lived by. "I again say I don't know the specifics. But I will. And when I do, I will act. And I can and do promise you this. I deal with my family members the same way I do strangers when it comes to guilt. If they're guilty, they will pay the price."

"Oh, give me a break."

"You think I can keep the peace in a kingdom like Zohayd by playing favorites? I am where I am, as effective as I am, because everyone knows my code and believes beyond a shadow of doubt that I would never compromise it. And I never do."

Her eyes flickered before they hardened again. "Good for you. But I'm not telling you anything more. What will you do? Force it out of me like those thugs intended to?"

He ached with the need to erase that doubt, that fear, once and forever. He couldn't bear that she could be uncertain of her fate with him. "I again swear that you are safe with me, in every way, no matter what."

His gaze bored into hers, as if he'd drive the conviction inside her mind with the force of his, until she gave an uncomfortable shrug.

He knew that was all the concession he'd get now.

He exhaled. "With that settled, let's get to other vital points. Now that I know you're not the reporter you were…reported to be, and not the spy I suspected you to be, I am wondering if all this isn't a case of catastrophic misinformation on all sides, if you weren't kidnapped for the wrong reasons."

She gave him an exasperated look. "Is that your round-about way to get to the reason I was taken, the same reason you came to extract me? Okay, let's get this out of the way. I came here following a lead that can prove my brother's innocence. And I stumbled on information terminally damaging to the Aal Shalaans. I have no idea how your rival tribe, or you for that matter, got wind of that, and so quickly. Maybe when I emailed my brother's attorney with the developments. So yes, I know why I was kidnapped. Your rival tribe wants the information I have to destroy you. You want it to avoid being destroyed."

And though she was looking at him as if she'd like nothing more than to see him and his family "destroyed," another wave of admiration surged inside him for this golden lioness who was here risking everything for her twin.

He at last sighed. "At least one thing turned out as I believed. But you said you were 'given' the chance to prove your brother's innocence and refused to tell me who gave it to you. Don't you realize that someone is orchestrating all this?"

A considering look came into her eyes. "Sure. Your point?"

"My point is, that someone cares nothing about you or your brother, you're just one of the instruments they're using to their end of causing the most chaos and destruction."

She gave a slow nod. "I never thought they were doing this out of the kindness of their hearts."

"Did they give you anything that might exonerate your brother yet?" She glared at him, then gave a grudging headshake. "Don't you find it suspicious they only gave you information that will hurt the Aal Shalaans?"

Her eyes spat blue fire. "According to them, it will end your reign."

He gritted his teeth at the very real danger of that coming to pass. "Didn't you ask yourself how they intend you to use that information? How using it will help your brother?"

She shrugged again, her eyes losing their hard gleam, the first flicker of uncertainty creeping there. "I didn't have time to think. I just got the info this morning, and within a couple of hours I was snatched. But I came to one decision. I wouldn't give my kidnappers anything. For every reason there is. I knew I wasn't walking out of that hole. So not only wasn't I about to be party to your tribal feud, I sure wasn't helping my abusers become the rulers of Zohayd and the abusers of millions."

He stared at her. There really was no end to her surprises. Almost anyone in her place would have said and given anything for a chance to walk away from the situation. But he'd pegged her right in those first moments. She *would* rather die in defiance, for a cause, than beg for her life from someone she despised and have her survival mean untold misery to others.

He fought the need to pull her into his arms, chide her for being such an obstinate hero. The one thing that stopped him, besides the settling weariness of the whole thing, was that he knew she'd resist. Spontaneous expression of emotion was something he'd have to work on re-earning.

He at last said, "You seem to realize the gravity of the information you have and what having it fall into the hands of the wrong people can mean. Have you decided what you'll do with it?"

Her shoulders drooped. "If I get out of this in one piece, you mean? I'll solidify my facts first. Then I'll think long and hard how best to use it." She shot him a sullen glance. "I may announce it to the world, maybe paving the way for Zohayd to become a democracy at last."

He raised both eyebrows, answering her surliness with sarcasm. "Like one of the so-called democracies in the region? *That* is the epitome of peace and prosperity, in your opinion? You want to save Zohayd from its current wealth and stability, from the hands of a royal family who have ruled it wisely and fairly for five hundred years and place it into the hands of hungry upstarts and militia warlords? And that's only Zohayd. Do you have the first inkling what the sprouting of such a 'democracy' among the neighboring monarchies would do? The unending repercussions it would send throughout the whole region?" He waited until he again found evidence of his points sinking home, in the darkness of grim realization in her eyes, the tremor of ominous possibilities in her lips. Then he went on, "Even if we're deposed tomorrow, and that doesn't plunge the region into chaos, it still doesn't help your brother. Or would you settle for avenging him, seeing his abusers punished, and leave him in prison for the rest of his sentence?"

"I don't know, okay?" she cried out, her eyes flaring her confusion and antipathy. "I told you, I had no time to think. And it's pointless to start right now. I'm in the middle of nowhere where I'm neither help nor threat to anyone. Ask me again, if I get out of this mess in any condition to be either."

Before he could assert that he would do anything to see her to safety, she winced, almost doubled over.

His heart folded in on itself, mimicking her contortion.

Before he could move, she keened, lurched back, and a ball of panic burst in his gut.

He'd taken her word that she was fine. What if he'd left an injury she'd sustained unseen to that long?

He pounced on her, disregarding the pain the careless move shot through his side. He raised her face to his, feverishly examining its locked-in-pain features.

It was only when she tried to escape his solicitous hands that he could rasp, "Talia, stop being stubborn, not about this. Are you injured?"

"No." He firmed his hold on her shoulder, on her head, detaining her with support and solicitude, demanding a confession. She groaned, relented. "It's those punches. Guess I was too distracted to focus on anything my body was feeling till now. But suddenly it...cramps with every breath. You know, like being cripplingly sore the morning after too many sit-ups." Something feral rolled out of his gut. Her eyes shot wider. Then she gave a huff that segued into a moan as her eyes slid down his body to his abdomen then back to his eyes. "What am I saying? It's sit-ups that are probably sore after a stint with your six-pack."

She was distracting him. Even thinking she owed him nothing but hostility, even if she wasn't acknowledging the sincerity of his outrage on her behalf, she was still trying to defuse it.

Before he kissed her, compelled her to carry out her earlier threat, he said, "Talia, I'm going to take off those layers of clothes..."

"Oh, no, you're not!" she squeaked.

"Then you do it. But I will have them off. Then you're going to lie down against me. You're going to stretch those muscles, or they're only going to get worse. I'll massage them with anti-inflammatory ointment."

She remained stiff in his hands for a moment longer before she capitulated, nodded and unzipped her coat.

He followed those capable hands as they undid the layers of clothes beneath it. And when he realized she wore a corset under her man's undershirt, he felt blood desert his head, his heart seeming to pump it only to his loins. He'd been in enough trouble when he'd believed her figure was as uneventful as a boy's. She'd been subduing a very... eventful one.

When she'd moved things around to expose only her midriff, she looked at him awkwardly. She tensed again when he began to turn her, and he whispered in her ear, "Let me take care of you. Don't resist me."

A breath shuddered out of her as she let him manipulate her body onto his lap. "Resistance is futile, huh?"

He smiled down at her as he opened the ointment tube. "Oh, yes. You're in no shape for it right now. Resist me all you like when you're no longer in pain."

She murmured something, a cross between grudging consent and whimpering pain/pleasure as he carefully began to examine her, then spread the ointment he'd warmed first between him palms over her aching flesh. His own flesh ached, too, all over.

Then, as she relaxed into his touch, arched up into his soothing hands, he saw the outline where the impact had bruised her paleness.

All blood was back, shooting into his head.

He heard the viciousness in his voice as he growled,

"Just thinking they had their hands on you at all, let alone in violence, makes me contemplate murder."

She fidgeted at his intensity, her eyes scanning him from her upside-down position. "You mean you don't do that on auto?"

He gave her a chiding glance. "Murder isn't even in the same solar system as manipulation or framing innocents for fraud. Don't you think you're taking your enmity too far?"

She sighed as she relaxed again under his cosseting hands. "I don't know. Maybe you think killing someone a suitable punishment for abusing their power, as an ultimate example for others. As for taking my enmity too far, let me throw one of your brothers in jail for five years, ruin his future and destroy his psyche, and then we'll discuss the exaggeration of my beliefs and reactions."

He stopped his massaging movements when she started to quiver. She could be getting cold or tender…or aroused. He was all of that. And though all he wanted was to rip off his clothes and hers and remedy all the causes of their distress, he knew that must remain a fantasy for now.

With what stood between them, maybe forever.

He kept his hands pressed lightly into her flesh for a few more defusing moments, his gaze tangling with her turbulent one.

Then he removed his hands, helped her up. She declined his help straightening her clothes. Then, with her eyes still wrestling with his, she nestled into the farthest part of the cockpit from him, against her door.

He'd thought he could postpone this until she was less raw, until he'd decided how to go on from here. But her withdrawal snapped something inside him. He had to settle this score. Now.

He pressed closer, showing her he wouldn't take her

categorizing him as the villain and shunning him. "Let's get one thing clear, Talia. *I* was not a party to what happened to your brother. So I have no more to say on this matter. And nothing to apologize for." Satisfaction surged as he saw that sense of fairness of hers flickering in her gaze, admitting his point. "So, until I'm in a position to learn more, and do something about it, I won't let you bring it up again. The subject of your brother is closed for now."

He held her eyes until she gave him a resentful if conceding huff.

He gave her an approving nod, as if sealing their treaty.

Then he said, "Now, to the only subject we should concern ourselves with for the duration. Our survival."

Five

"What do you mean *our* survival?"

Harres frowned at Talia's glower. His was of confusion. Hers seemed to be equal measures that and a revival of anger.

"What kind of a question is that? We're in the middle of nowhere, as you pointed out. The most hostile nowhere on the planet."

"Yeah, sure. So?"

He shook his head, as if it would shake her words into making sense. "You were worried about getting out of this alive. I thought you understood the danger we're in."

"I thought *I* was in danger. The only danger I thought I was in was human-induced."

His exasperation rose to match hers. "You mean *me*-induced."

She shrugged, unfazed by his displeasure. "Yeah, you-induced. I was thinking you'd use my being out here with you as the only way of rejoining humanity, as…persuasion to get me to spill. And that once you were certain I wouldn't give you anything, you wouldn't be too gung ho about my well-being, maybe even my survival."

Blood bounded in his arteries until he felt each hammer against the confines of his body.

He forcibly exhaled frustration before he burst with it. "I thought we got this ridiculous—and let me add, most dishonoring, injuring and aggravating—misconception out of the way."

Her eyes seemed to be giving him a total mind-and-psyche scan before she gave a slow nod. "I guess so. But since that only happened in the past few minutes, I had no time to form an alternate viewpoint. I sure didn't consider for a second that you were in any danger. After the escape, the gunshot and the crash, that is. After you survived all that in one glorious piece, I thought you were home free."

"How is it even possible you think so?"

"Oh, I don't know." Her voice drenched him in sarcasm. "Maybe my first clue was how glib about the whole situation you were. You know, being so cheerful and carefree that you spent most of the past hour laughing and lobbing witticisms in between pestering me for my gender, interrogating me for my agenda and trying to deluge me with testosterone."

And he had to. He laughed again. "It's your effect on me. You make me cheerful and carefree, against all odds."

Her lips crooked up in a goading smile. "Next you'll say I made you kiss me."

"In a fashion. You made me unable to draw one more breath if I didn't. You made me thankful. That I found you, that I saved you, that you saved me, that you exist and that you're with me. And you did make me do it in the most important way, the way all of the above still couldn't have made me. Because you wanted me to."

She gave her lips, which had fallen open, an involuntary lick, her eyes glittering as if she felt his there, tasted him. Then she gave a smothered, chagrined sound before her eyes sharpened again and she thrust both hands at him in a fed-up gesture. "See? Is it any wonder I couldn't even conceive that you had anything to worry about? Who talks like that if he's in any kind of danger, let alone a potentially life-threatening situation?"

He sighed, conceding her point. "Apparently, I do. With you around. But when you talked about my needing your scalpels again, I thought that proved you were aware that I shared your danger."

She waved a hand. "Oh, I was just pointing out that if you held me here at your mercy, you'd be at mine, too."

He huffed a stunned chuckle. "We're sitting inside a crashed helicopter, *our* as well as *my* only way out of here. How can you consider that I'm not right with you at the mercy of the desert?"

Her shrug was defensive this time. "Why should I have considered that? So the helicopter crashed. But you're the one, the only, Prince Harres Aal Shalaan. You must have all sorts of gadgets on hand and can contact your people to come pick you up whenever you want."

He gave a regretful nod. "I do have gadgets, every one known to humankind. And all useless, since we are in a signal blackout zone. The nearest area with possibility of transmitting or receiving anything is over two hundred miles away."

Her eyes widened with each word until they'd expanded to a cartoonish exaggeration. "You mean your people have no way of knowing where you are?

"None."

After a moment of wrestling with descending dread, she seemed to come to a conclusion that steadied her. "Well, that alone will have your armies combing the desert to find you."

"Sure it will." He sighed in resignation. "And they'll find me. In maybe a week. We have water on board for a couple of days."

"They can't possibly take a week to find you!" Her protest came out a squeak. "With all the high-end tech stuff at their disposal, and the whole country out looking for its precious prince, I bet they find you within a couple of hours from the moment they realize you're missing!"

He wanted to press her into his flesh and absorb her worry. But he owed her the truth. He would see her to safety, but he had to prepare her for the grueling experience that he couldn't spare her before he did.

Bleakness clamped his heart, erasing any lightness as he forced himself to decimate her hope. "They have no way of knowing where to start looking. Once my men go back home and realize I didn't precede them, they'll go back to where we originally landed as a starting point to search. But they'll have no way of knowing which way I headed, or how far in which direction I crashed."

"So they'd take longer, maybe a day or two," she still argued. "Surely they'll crisscross the area with enough aircrafts, one of them is bound to spot us within that time frame."

He shook his head, needing to erase any false expectations. Those were more damaging than painful reality. "Relying on visual search over an area of a hundred thousand square miles? With some of the dunes around here over one thousand feet high? Apart from a stroke of luck, I was being optimistic when I said a week."

Silenced howled after his last word.

She stared at him with horror gathering in her eyes.

Then it burst from her lips. "Oh, *God*. You're stranded here with me."

He couldn't hold back any longer. He reached out and cupped her velvet cheek in soothing cherishing. "And I couldn't have dreamed of better company to be in mortal danger with."

Her mouth opened, closed, then again. She couldn't have looked more flabbergasted if he'd said he was actually a plant.

Then she slapped his hand away with a furious sound. "How can you joke about this now? About anything?"

"I'm not joking in the least." He reached out to her again and she snapped her teeth at him like the infuriated feline she was. He withdrew his hand with a sigh. "You can chomp any part of me you like, but it won't change the fact that what I said is the truth. Apart from not wishing you to be in any discomfort or danger, there's no one else I'd rather have with me now."

Tears suddenly eddied in a swirl of silver in her eyes, had his blood churning in his heart before two arrowed down her cheeks.

Then she choked out, "Oh, shut *up!*"

He hooted with laughter. "And you take me to task about being cheerful? I'd be mute if you had your way, wouldn't I?"

She shot him a baleful glance, even as her lips twitched, too. "You've said enough, don't you think?"

"Actually, I was getting to the interesting part."

"What interesting part? How after a few millennia they'll dig our bones from this desert and put them in an exhibit and have scientists hypothesizing that we were actually Adam and Eve?"

He dug his fingers into his seat so he wouldn't yank her to him and claim those lips under his. "How...anthropologically imaginative of you. But I have no intention of becoming a fossil just yet. To this end, we'll have to get out of this hunk of twisted metal and have us a desert trek."

She said nothing. Then she shifted, came closer and patted her lap. "You should lie down again. It's clear you did hit your head and everything you've said and done so far has originated from a swollen brain."

His eyes laughed into her in-doctor-mode ones. "You mean you don't think I have one by default?"

"Sure, as is no doubt expected of your princeliness. But when you start suggesting we take a two-hundred-mile stroll in 'the most hostile nowhere on the planet,' it's time for medical intervention."

"Actually, it's only a fifty-mile stroll. That's the distance to the oasis I was taking us to when we had this little diversion."

He winced inwardly at the hope that swept her ultra-expressive features, rearranging them into the image of relief, then reprimand. "Why didn't you say so? That's not too far."

"That's two marathons' worth. In the desert. With temperatures reaching 120 degrees Fahrenheit at midday and 20 at night. And that's if we're talking a linear path to our destination, which we're not. Not with the seas of dry quicksand in the way."

She raised her chin defiantly at him. "If you're trying to scare me, save it. I didn't come to Zohayd from an air-conditioned exam room in a five-star hospital, but from an understaffed and hectic emergency room in a teaching hospital and a couple of aid stints in Africa. I've been steeped in discomfort all my working years and I've rubbed shoulders with danger and despair quite a few times, by choice."

He had to pause to admire her for a moment before he

said, "I'm only trying to prepare you. I'll see that we get through this, in the most efficient way possible, but I need you to be aware of the facts. So far, we've gone through the easy part. Now we face the desert."

He could see her defiance and determination wavering, uncertainty and fear skirting their protective shell, scraping against it for chinks, for a way in.

But the good thing about challenge was that it kept one focused. Maybe he should escalate it, keep all her faculties locked on it, and on him.

He crooked his lips, knowing by now that would stoke her ready flames. "Anyway, great to know I won't have a swooning damsel on my hands."

"As long as I don't have a swooning dude on mine!"

There she was. Ricocheting right back at him. And he laughed again, shook his head at his helpless reaction.

They were in a demolished multimillion-dollar helicopter in what might as well be another planet for all the area's desolation. He was going to brave the desert's mercilessness in his weakened condition to ensure her safety. She seemed to wish him and his whole family erased from the face of the earth.

And yet, he had never enjoyed anything as much, never looked forward to anything more.

But though he did, and had said they'd focus on their current predicament, he couldn't forget the beef she had with his family. An unjustly imprisoned sibling was the stuff of undying grudges.

This *was* worse than anything he'd imagined. He'd thought he'd be bargaining with a news bounty hunter or an intel black marketer. But he couldn't have imagined this. Imagined her. What she was, how she affected him, what she had against his family.

Even the response he wrenched from her was one more strike against him.

Not that he'd let this, or anything, stand in his way.

He wanted her to give him everything. The info. And herself.

He always got what he wanted.

And he'd never known he *could* want like this.

Everything she knew, felt, was, had to be his. *Would* be his.

He cocked his head and her gaze slid unwilling admiration and sensuality over the hair that fell to his shoulder.

Pleasure revved inside his chest. "Now we're squared on that, how about shelving your enmity until we survive this?"

"*You're* only playing nice because you need *me*. Primary closure of a wound of that caliber is in four to ten days."

He knew that. He also knew she needed to provoke him to keep her spirits up. He let her. "And *you* need *me*. You won't find any passersby here to hitch a ride with to the nearest oasis. So how about *you* be nice to *me?*"

Her eyes stormed through vexation, futility and resignation before she harrumphed. "Okay, okay. I concede the need is mutual."

"It is. In every way. Even if you're too mad right now to concede that."

She blasted him with a glare of frustration. He only grinned and dueted her exasperated, "Oh, shut *up.*"

Six

No one could know how absolutely majestic and humbling night could be until they'd been in the desert at night.

Problem was, it was also downright petrifying and alien.

Talia had known they were in the middle of nowhere. But before she got out of the helicopter, that had only been a concept, a figure of speech. Now it was reality. One that impacted her every sense and inundated her every perception. As she at last had the chance to appreciate.

And what a vantage she had to appreciate it from.

Harres had crash-landed them about five dozen feet from the top of one of those thousand-foot dunes he'd spoken of. From this spot she had an almost unlimited view of the tempestuous oceans of sand that seemed to simmer with their own arcane energy, emit their own indefinable color and eerie illumination. At the edge of her vision, they pushed in a scalpel-sharp demarcation against a dome of deepest eternity scattered with stars, the unblinking shrapnel of the big boom. Under their omnidirectional light, each steep undulation created occult shadows that seemed to metamorphose into shapes, entities. Some seemed to look back at her, some seemed to beckon, some to crawl closer. It made her realize how Middle Eastern fables had come to such vivid and sometimes macabre life. She certainly felt as if a genie or worse would materialize at any time.

Then again, she'd already met her genie.

Right now, he was taking apart the mangled rear of the helicopter to get to the gear and supplies they'd need before they set off on their oasis-bound trek.

She shuddered again, this time complete with chattering teeth, as much from expanding awe and descending dread as from marrow-chilling cold aided by a formidable windchill factor.

Though he was making a racket cutting the twisted metal with shears he'd retrieved from the cockpit, and the wind had risen again, eddying laments around them, it seemed he'd heard her.

He straightened with a groan that reminded her of his injury, made her wonder again how he ignored it, functioned—and so efficiently—with only the help of a painkiller shot.

He reached out to her face, cupped her cheek in the coolness of his huge, calloused hand and frowned. "You're freezing. Go back to the cockpit."

She shook her head. "I'm cold, yes, freezing, no. You're the one who's half-dressed."

Her last word got mangled by another teeth-rattling shiver.

His scowl deepened. "We need to set some ground rules. When I say something, you obey. I'm your commanding officer here."

She stuck her fists at her waist. "We're not in your army and I'm not one of your soldiers."

He fixed her with an adamant glare of his own. "I'm the native around here. And I'm the leader of this expedition."

"I thought we agreed we have equal billing."

"We do. In our respective areas of expertise."

"And you're the desert knight, right?"

He gave her a mock-affronted look, palm over his chest. "What? I don't look the part?"

"You sure do." *With a capital T in "the,"* she added inwardly. "But we established that looks can be deceiving."

"I thought *I* established they can't be."

"So you're the real thing. But you could be the prototype and this would remain *my* area. I'm the one qualified to judge which one of us is in danger of hypothermia. And until you get bundled up in thermal clothing like I am, that's you. So now you've done your Incredible Hulk bit and torn away debris and cleared a path to our supplies, you go back to the cockpit. I'll get the stuff we need."

He took a challenging step, crowding her against the mangled hull. "You'd spend hours trying to figure out what is where. I'm the one who knows where the stuff we'll need is, and can get it in minutes. If you can stop arguing that long."

"So I'm the uninjured, suitably dressed one, and your doctor, but you're the expert on this lost-cause aircraft and on survival in the desert. See? We end up with equal billing. So we both stay, work together and cut the effort and time in half."

His eyes had been following her mouth, explicit with thoughts of stopping it with his lips. And teeth.

Then he raised them to hers and captured her in that

bedeviling appreciation she was getting dangerously used to. "You're a control freak, aren't you?"

She let her shoulders rise and drop nonchalantly. "Takes one to know one, eh?"

His lips widened in a heart-palpitating grin. "You bet."

And even though she'd been and still was in mortal danger, and the emergency light at his feet cast sinister shadows over his hewn face, as if exposing some supernatural entity lurking inside him, she couldn't remember a time when she'd felt more...energized.

Strange how the company made all the difference when the situation remained the same.

I couldn't have dreamed of better company to be in mortal danger with.

Yeah, what he'd said.

Not that she'd agreed to it then. Or could credit it now. But there it was. She was actually looking forward to the grueling and possibly life-threatening time ahead. She'd always thrived on challenge and hardship to start with, but she'd never been anywhere near that level of danger. With Harres by her side, anything felt possible. And doable. And anything was...enjoyable?

She shook her head, as if she could dislodge the ridiculous thought. How could anything be enjoyable in their situation?

She had no idea how. But having no rationalization didn't change the fact that being with him was turning this nightmare into the most stimulating experience of her life.

She watched as he bent the last strip of protruding metal, widening the makeshift hatch, then stepped back, gestured to her.

"Report to packing duty, my obdurate dew droplet."

Her heart punched her ribs. No one, not even her parents,

had ever come up with such endearments for her. Nothing anywhere as ready and inventive and…sweet. A woman could get used to this.

And this woman shouldn't. For every reason there was.

She bit down on the bubble of delight rising inside her, popped it.

"That's your retaliation for pigheaded, mulish ox and my assortment of other insults?" she tossed over her shoulder as she preceded him into the cramped space, kneeled on the uneven floor of what remained of the cargo bay and awaited his directions.

He came down facing her, started reaching for articles as if he knew exactly where they were. And he clearly did. Prince Harres seemed to be hands-on in his operations' every level and detail.

After he hoisted on a thermal jacket, he answered her previous barb. "I am sabotaging myself by telling you this, since you might now stop them, but those aren't insults. From you, they have the effect of the most…intimate caress."

His eyes left her in no doubt of what that meant. She almost choked her lungs out imagining his body stirring, hardening, aching in response to her words, to her…

She pretended to cough, waved a hand at him. "Try another one. You're just insult-proof, as you said early on."

"You remember?" He looked disproportionately pleased that she did. "*Aih,* I've never had a hair-trigger ego. And then, most insults are falsehoods or exaggerations, attempts to get a rise. My best payback to insults is to let them slide off me, inside and out."

She gasped in mock stupefaction. "You mean people actually dare to attempt to insult you?"

"I have an older brother. A very…aggravating one. And three younger ones. I'm no stranger to insults. But you will insult me only if you fear me or distrust me."

Her heart hiccuped at the sudden seriousness in his eyes. The cross between warning and entreaty there had the mocking comeback sticking in her throat. She instinctively knew he was telling the truth. That this was the one thing he wouldn't laugh at. The one thing that would hurt him.

And even if she told herself Todd's ordeal balanced out everything Harres had done for her, that he'd only done it for the person who held the vital info he wanted to extract and to keep hushed, her fairness again intervened. He'd been right when he'd said he had nothing to do with Todd's imprisonment. And she didn't believe in guilt by association, even if she made it sound as if she did. And if she went a step further into truthfulness, she had to admit something else.

She didn't want to hurt him. Not in any way.

Lowering her gaze in indirect agreement and swallowing her barbed tongue, she helped him drag out backpacks then cut off the safety belts that still secured crates in the debris.

He dragged one between them, popped the lid open before looking at her with teasing back in his eyes, to her relief. "There's one thing I can't get over. How you don't take words lauding your beauty and effect as your due—my jasmine dew."

She followed his lead, loaded water bottles and packets of dry food into the backpacks. "Next you'll call me Mountain Dew."

A chuckle rumbled inside his massive chest. "Oh, no. You get your own brand names. But we do have canned relatives around."

She stuffed a compartment into one backpack, turned

to the other one, which she noticed was much smaller, as he pulled out another crate. "How nutritionally sloppy of you."

He opened the crate, produced guns, flares, flashlights, batteries, compasses and many other articles, which he distributed between the two backpacks. "I assure you, I never come within a mile of anything canned, except in emergencies. For easily stored quick fixes of hydration and calories, they work in a bind."

"Let's hope we don't have to resort to them. I'd rather drink detergent. But then we won't have to, since you have it all figured out, being the desert knight that you are."

He gave her a stoking glance. "That's right. And this desert knight says close your backpack and let's move on to packing our accommodations."

"You mean this tiny thing is mine?" She eyed his backpack. It was almost as big as her. "And this behemoth is yours?"

He nodded matter-of-factly. "I am twice as big as you are, and can carry four times as much or more."

"Listen, this is getting old. I won't stand by while you bust my sutures."

"I thought they were mine." Before the urge to smack him transferred from her brain to her arm, he added, "If I can't handle it, I'll tell you."

"Yeah, right. Right after you tell me you've sighted the first flying pig."

"But I'm the mulish ox here, therefore perfectly qualified for hefting and towing." Before she could plow into a counterargument, he cupped her face in both hands. The gentleness in his grasp made everything inside her crumple, pour into those palms. "Thank you for worrying about me, for braving exhaustion to spare me. But I've been through worse, have trained to weather the worst conditions for over a quarter of a century." His lips quirked. "Probably longer than you've been on the planet."

That shook her out of her hypnosis. "What? When I told you I've been practicing medicine for years? You think they grant babies medical licenses now?"

"They do, to prodigies."

"Well, I'm not one. I'll be thirty next August."

"No way." He looked genuinely stunned.

"Yes way."

"See? No end to your surprises."

"Stick around. They're bound to end sometime."

"Oh, I intend to. And I bet they never will."

"Didn't take you for a betting man."

"I'm not. But I'll bet on you anytime."

Only then did she notice he still held her face in his palms. And that she was shaking all over again. And that he knew that he turned her into a live wire, knew she was struggling not to succumb. He was also certain she would.

She glared back. *Never again.*

"Don't be so sure," he murmured, his tone a sweeping undertow, his exotic accent sliding over her, enveloping her.

She gasped. He'd heard her thoughts, was taking the challenge.

She shook her head, reclaimed her face from his possession.

With a last molten look of challenge, he resumed packing.

Afterward, he fashioned a sled from the helicopter's remains, using ropes for a harness. On it he loaded a folded tent, their quarters, as he called it, and piled on blankets, sleeping bags and mats.

She matched him move for move, followed his directions,

anticipating his needs as if they'd been working together for years in perfect harmony. And she felt that overwhelming in-sync feeling again, just as she'd felt when he'd assisted her in treating his wound, always reading her next move, ready for it with the most efficient action.

It wasn't only that. She felt her body gravitating toward him, demanding his closeness. She resisted the compulsion with an equal force until she felt she'd rip down the middle.

It's survival, she told herself. Seeking the one person around. Being out here would have been unsettling enough in controlled conditions. But she'd just learned that her predicament was far worse than she'd thought. And with him generating that field of reassurance and invincibility, who could blame her if all she wanted was to throw herself into his haven?

And since when did she indulge in self-deception?

This man had jolted things inside her, like electric cables forced life into a dead battery, from the second she'd turned to face him. Ever since, his nearness, everything he said or did, revved that life into something almost…painful. An edge that scraped everything aside. A knot of hunger that—

"You're hungry."

She jerked at the dark compulsion of his voice, and glared her resentment at him. Couldn't he have the decency to have one crack in his imperturbable facade? It might be self-defeating to wish that her one chance at survival be less than the absolute rock he needed to be to get them out of this, but she still wished it. No one could be *that* unflappable, could he?

He only looked at her with that boundless tranquility that she felt traversed his being. She answered her own question.

Yes, someone could be. And his name was Harres Aal Shalaan.

And he'd just read her mind. Again.

Before mortification choked her, he let her off the hook. "Like you, your stomach snaps its teeth." And she realized it was. She hadn't eaten in over twenty-four hours. "So here's the plan. We eat, prepare our gear then move out. It's 1:00 a.m. now. If we move out in an hour, we'll have around eight hours before things get too hot. When it does, we'll set up camp, hide out the worst of it, then set out again before sunset. The schedule throughout will be two hours on, one hour off. More off if you need it. At a rate of about five miles every three hours, we'll make it to our destination in about three days. If we ration ourselves, our supplies should last."

"If they don't, I'll use the IV fluid replacement. We have a few liters still."

"See? You *are* the best I could have hoped to be with in this mess."

"I'm sure you could have managed on your own," she mumbled, thrilled, annoyed, feeling things were about to get real at last, and struggling not to throw herself into his arms and cling.

"You're admitting I'm not a useless nuisance? I'm deeply honored."

She studied him for a moment, a suspicion coming over her.

Was he doing this on purpose? Every time she felt her will flagging, he teased her or provoked her and it brought her out of her funk and right back in his face.

Whatever it was, it was working. She grabbed at it with both hands. "It remains to be seen what exactly you are. You might still take us in the wrong direction and we'll end up lost. And fossilized."

He laughed. Rich, virile, mind-numbing laughter. Made all the more hard-hitting as it mixed with a guttural groan of pain. "I don't take wrong directions. It's a matter of principle."

Yeah. She'd bet. And she was willing to gamble her life on that. She was going to.

Then again, what choice did she have?

None.

But then again, why should she even worry?

He'd gotten her this far, through impossible odds.

If there was anyone in this world who could get them through this, it was him.

But what if there was no getting through it...?

He suddenly grabbed her hand and yanked her against him.

This time she met him more than halfway. As he'd told her she would.

And whether it was survival, magic, compulsion, or anything else, she needed it. He needed it. She let them have it.

She dissolved in the maddening taste of him deep inside her, with the thrust of his hot velvet tongue as he breached her with tenderness and carnality and desperation. She surrendered to his domination and supplication, all-consuming and life-giving.

Then he wrenched away, held her head, her eyes. "I said you were safe with me, Talia, in every way. I'll keep you safe, and I'll see you safe. This is a promise. Tell me you believe me."

She did. And she told him. "I believe you."

Seven

Talia wondered, for the thousandth time since she'd been snatched from her rented condo at gunpoint, if any of the things that had happened since could be real.

One thing was certain, though. Harres was.

And she was following him across an overwhelmingly vast barren landscape that made her feel like one of the sand particles shifting like solid fluid beneath her feet.

They'd set out over six hours ago. Before they had, during the hour Harres had specified for preparations, he'd studied the stars and his compass at length, explaining how he was combining their codes with his extensive knowledge of his land's terrain and secrets to calculate their course. He'd said he needed her to know all he did. She thought that impossible when she couldn't imagine how he fathomed different landmarks when sameness besieged them. Yet he'd insisted it was vital she visualize their path, too, and somehow managed to transmit it to her.

They'd just embarked on their third two-hour hike. He still walked ahead, seemingly effortlessly, carrying his mammoth backpack and towing the piled sled while she stumbled in his wake with her fraction of their load. Which was still surprisingly heavy. He'd been keeping them on paths of firm sand, so it wasn't too hard. At first. She'd soon had to admit anything heavier would have been a real struggle.

She still continuously offered to carry more. Each time he'd answered that silence would boost their aerobic efficiency and increased the steps he kept between them no matter how hard she tried to catch up with him. It wasn't only adamant chivalry, it felt as if he was making sure he would be the first to face whatever surprises the seemingly inanimate-since-creation desert brought, wouldn't let her take a step before he'd ascertained its safety, testing it with his own.

Acknowledging his protection and honoring it, she treaded the oceans of granulated gold in the imprints of his much larger feet, feeling as if she was forging a deeper connection with him with each step, gaining a more profound insight into what made this unprecedented—and no doubt unduplicable—man tick.

It had been hours since dawn had washed away the stars and their inky canvas, the gradual boost in illumination bringing with it an equally relentless rise in temperature. While that had made each step harder than the last, it had given her a new distraction to take her mind off counting them, off the weakness invading her limbs.

He'd shed one layer of clothing after another, was now down to the bandages she'd changed an hour ago and the second-skin black pants fitted into black leather boots. With his back to her, she was finally free to study him, to realize something.

He was perfect.

No, beyond that. Not only couldn't she find fault with him, but the more she scrutinized, the more details she found to marvel at.

He seemed to be encased in molten bronze spun into polished satin ingeniously accentuated by dark silk. His proportions were a masterpiece of balance and harmony, a study in strength and grandeur. She'd never thought a man of such height and muscular bulk and definition could display such grace, such finesse, such poise. How could such a staggeringly physical manifestation combine such power and poetry of motion? And that was when he was half-buried under the backpack and tethered with the sled's harness. *And* that was only his body.

His face was a testimony to divine taste, hewn beauty in planes and slashes of perfection. In the dimness, his eyes had dominated her focus, but now, as she saw his face from every possible angle, she found something new to appreciate with every self-possessed move of his head. Between the intelligence stamped on the width of a leonine forehead, the distinct cut of razor-sharp cheekbones, the command in the jut of a sculpted jaw and nose and the humor and passion molding sense-scrambling lips, she couldn't form an opinion on a favorite feature. Not when so many other things vied for her favor. The eyebrows, the lashes, the neck, even the ears.

And then there was the hair.

Since dawn's first silvery fingers had touched it, she'd become fascinated with it. But it had taken full exposure to the desert's merciless sun to highlight its wonders.

The color seemed to have been painted from a palette of every earth color in creation, forged from resilient gloss and blended with trapped solar energy. As he walked ahead, the undulating silk seemed an extension of his beauty and virility, transmitting the same power and purpose. Every few minutes, when he turned to check on her, the mass seemed to beckon to her numb fingers to come revel in its pleasures for themselves.

Just then he turned to her again, and that curtain of luxury swished around, catching the nine-o'clock sun, leaving her gulping down her heart. And that was before he gave her that look, that amalgam of encouragement, solicitude and challenge that injected willpower into her veins and pumped it to her limbs. And she realized something.

This was what the Prince of Darkness should look like. To seduce without trying, to enslave into eternity, to induce all sorts of unrepentant sins. To have a woman believe her soul was a trivial accessory.

And she must be starting to hallucinate from exhaustion.

Maybe she should call another time-out before she collapsed.

Problem was, she was exhausted, but nowhere near collapse. Which meant all those thoughts were originating from an unwarped mind.

She tore her eyes away from his hypnotic movements, tried to document the subtle yet rich changes every mile brought to the awesome desert terrain. This place might be a trekker's nightmare, but it was any geologist's, artist's, or nature-lover's dream.

There was so much to delight in as the landscape shifted from magnificent sand dunes to endless gravel-covered plains to sinuous dry lakebeds and stream channels and back again to dunes. The sky, too, transformed from a fathomless ink canopy studded with faraway infernos to a stratus-painted, multicolored canvas to a blazing azure void as the sun rose and incinerated all in its path.

As the heat and glare intensified, she felt so thankful

for the sunglasses he'd had on board—the one undamaged pair that he'd insisted she have—and the cool cotton cloth he'd fashioned into a head cover for her.

At 10:00 a.m. sharp, he stopped.

Though all she wanted was to sit down and never rise again, when he turned to her she rasped, "I can go on."

He shook his head and took off his harness and bag. "No use going farther only to exhaust you so you'll need longer to rest. Or worse, be unable to go on altogether."

"You're the one with the gunshot wound. And I'm used to being on my feet for days on end in my work."

He only took her bag, his smile adamant. "You've gone through the equivalent of four of your grueling days in the last twelve hours." Before she could protest again he overrode her. "But since it's against your principles to be catered to, you can help me set up the tent."

She nodded reluctantly. She was dying to rest, but she wanted to get this trek over with more.

He handed her the tent. Then she found out why he'd offered it to her. Because he knew there was nothing for her to really do. Once she unfolded the thing, it sprang into existence with very little adjustment.

After gathering supplies for the next hours, he led her inside and she was even more impressed. It was big enough to accommodate ten people, and he could stand erect inside it. The sand-colored fabric was tough and cool, the floor's insulation total, the openings sealed once zipped and the ventilation ingenious.

But it was still hot. Too hot. And most of the heat was being generated by her smoldering hunk of a companion.

She looked up from gulping water and found him staring down at her with eyes that flared and subsided like fanned coals.

"Take off your clothes."

She jerked at his dark murmur, a geyser of heat shooting from her recesses to flood her skin.

His eyes left hers, traveled down, as if looking for the origin of the flush that rose to take over her neck and face.

And that was before he added in a will-numbing whisper, "All of them."

She stared at him, at a loss for the first time since she'd seen him. This was the last thing she...she...

Then his lips twitched, one corner twisting up devilishly, belying the seriousness in his voice when he elaborated, "If you don't, you'll sweat liters we can't replace."

Oh. Of course. She bit her lower lip, nodded, dispersing the ridiculous alarm and temptation that had slammed into her.

Problem was, in a usual "all of them" clothes-removal scenario she would have kept her underwear on, which would have amounted to a conservative bikini. But with only a man's undershirt over her now undone corsets, she'd be down to her boxer shorts. And she didn't know what mortified her more. That he'd see her topless, or that he'd see how ridiculous she looked in them.

Oh, right. And that was grounds for risking dehydration?

She nodded, exhaled a tremulous breath. "Any hope you'll turn your back?"

He gave her a mock-innocent look. "Why?"

Then he began to take off what little clothes he had left. He started with yanking off his boots, then straightening to undo the fastening of his pants. Her eyes were glued to his every move, her tongue darting to moisten suddenly desiccated lips. It was only when she realized her eyes were sliding lower with her mouth open as she anticipated the big revelation that she felt fury spurt to douse her mortification and abort her daze.

She met the master-tormentor's gaze defiantly, then started to undress herself. If he thought she'd swoon at the sight of his endowments, that she'd turn around for modesty or try to shield her nudity with virginly arms, he could think again!

As she prepared to yank off the short-sleeved undershirt, Harres stretched and manipulated something at the ceiling. A heavy cloth partition snapped down between them.

She froze, staring at the opaque surface inches from her eyes, until his amused drawl from the other side roused her.

"I did say 'quarters,' plural."

And she cried, "You…you…weasel!"

"Now we move from the farm to the animal kingdom at-large."

The mixture of relief and chagrin choked her as she threw off the rest of her clothes to the sound of his teasing chuckles and tackled her thin matttress as if it were him.

But if she'd thought she'd toss and turn with him inches from her with only flimsy fabric between them, she was mistaken. She felt nothing from the moment she became horizontal, to the moment she came to. To his caresses.

She blinked up in confusion. He was kneeling beside her, running his hands gently over her hair and face and arms.

For a long moment she could only think what a wonderful way this was to wake up.

Then the wonder factor rose exponentially when he smiled down at her. "I called. And called. I even poked you through the partition, to no avail."

She blinked again, looked down, found herself covered in a light cotton blanket. But since he was the one who'd covered her, he must have seen everything. Still, he had covered her so that he wouldn't infringe on her. She struggled with the urge to throw her arms around him and bring him down to her, thank him for being so thoughtful. And more.

Instead, she croaked, "What time is it?"

"Sunset."

She jackknifed up in alarm. "But we were supposed to move out two hours ago!"

"You needed to rest. Now we'll move faster." Before she could reprimand him for not sticking to their schedule on account of her alleged delicacy, he ruffled her hair and winked. "Hop to it, my dewy doc."

She huffed as her heart fired against her ribs. He was suddenly treating her like his kid sister. And it *still* turned her insides into a mushy mess.

As she began to reach for her clothes, he turned back to her.

He took her undershirt away from a hand gone lax. He pulled it over her head, guided her flaccid arms through it, managing not to drop the blanket from where it covered her breasts. He drew it away only once the undershirt was securely in place.

Just when she thought she might suffer a coronary, his intent and serious expression turned incandescent with a surge of something dark and driven. Then he leaned down, opened his lips over the junction of her neck and shoulder.

The feel of his tongue and teeth there was like being prodded by lightning. She lurched under the force of sensations that thundered through her. Then he made it worse.

He glided to the tip of her shoulder, scraping her flesh

with his teeth, gathering the sweat beaded on it with his tongue.

He growled against her skin, sending a string of shock waves through her with every syllable.

She thought he said, "A reward…an incentive…"

Then he pulled back and disappeared into his compartment.

She flopped onto her back, gasping, before she forced herself up and into her clothes. Then she crawled to his side to check his wound before they resumed their grueling trek.

She'd have hours to contemplate the meaning of his words.

And the feelings he'd ripped from her depths.

By the end of the second day, their water supply had dwindled even though they drank only when absolutely necessary. They were losing gallons in this weather and with the exertion.

After midnight they stopped for their hour's rest.

As she drank, she noticed he didn't. She stopped, insisting he drink, that he was the one losing the most fluids handling ten times the weight she was. He only insisted on taking her up on her offer of IV fluids.

He hung the saline bag on his jacket so that she wouldn't have to stand and hold it for him. She protested the inefficiency of this maneuver, and he calmly unrolled a mat from the sled, propped it against the sloping edge of a dune, tossed a few blankets beside it, then caught her hand and pulled her down on it with him.

Before she knew what hit her, Harres was lounging with his back to the dune, his endless legs open with her between them, her hips in their V, her back to his chest, her head on his right shoulder. Then he cocooned them both in the blankets and crossed his arms over her midriff, plastering her to him.

After the first stunned moment, she tried to fidget away.

He tightened his hold, groaned in her ear, "Relax."

Relax? Was he insane?

And he wasn't only that, he was rubbing his lips against the top of her head, inhaling her and rumbling enjoyment as he talked. "Rest. Get warm. It's far colder than yesterday."

"W-we have enough blankets," she protested weakly. "We can roll in them separately."

"This *is* the best method of body temperature preservation."

"And to think I reminded you of that!"

His chuckle, reverberating beneath her ear, sent more waves of distress crashing through her. "Conserve your energy, my Talia. Sleep, and I'll wake you up in an hour, maybe two."

"I—I don't want to sleep."

"I don't either. I'd rather be awake, experiencing this with you."

And though she was far from cold, a tremor rattled through her.

He'd just put into words what she felt.

Though his arms were pressing beneath her suddenly aching breasts and her buttocks were pressed to what she suspected, if couldn't credit, was a massive erection, it wasn't sexual. Or not only so. She'd never felt this close to anyone. This intimate. Even during her now almost-forgotten sexual encounters, she hadn't been any closer to experiencing what she did with Harres than she was to one of the stars above.

She sighed, feeling as if her bones had turned to warm

liquid and the rest of her senses had melted in the sluggish heat of her blood. "Stars. They *are* still up there."

He nuzzled her cheek with his lips. "You don't see them much where you live, eh?"

She sighed in deeper contentment. "Make that don't see them at all. Not for years. But even when I did, I never saw so many. I didn't think there *were* so many. Scientifically speaking, I know there are endless numbers of them in our galaxy alone. But I never thought we could actually see them. There are millions of them."

Her voice sounded intoxicated to her ears. And she was. With the overpowering mixture of the virility enfolding her and the desert's magnificent menace.

His voice poured directly through to her brain, frying more synapses. "Actually, only about eight thousand are visible to us poor earthlings in any given hemisphere, no matter how clear the skies are. And you won't find any clearer anywhere in the world."

That piece of info she hadn't known. She turned in his arms languidly, looked up at him. "Don't tell me you counted them."

"I tried. Then had to borrow good scientists' findings."

"They seem so much more. But I'll take your word for it. I'm just glad they all showed up tonight."

"I ordered them to be present especially for you."

Coming from any other man, that would have sounded like an outrageous—and annoying as hell—line. But somehow, from Harres, this force of nature who seemed to be as one with the powers of this land, *his* land, it didn't seem far-fetched. She did feel as if he had an empathy, an understanding with their surroundings, as if they let him divine their secrets and share their strengths. And then, coming from the man who'd risked his life to save her, who'd lavished such care on her, showed her such admiration and restraint and solicitude, she could easily believe his wish to please her, to gift her. So even the sentiment behind the claim seemed right, sincere. Profound.

And if an inner voice told her it was his need to learn her secrets that fueled all of the above, she couldn't listen. No one could be that good at hiding ulterior motives. And she had experienced him through the worst that could be thrown at a person. He'd shone through with gallantry and resourcefulness, with kindness and control.

She at last sighed again. "I wouldn't put it past you. So they're your subjects, too?"

"Oh, no. They're just old friends. We have an understanding."

Just as she'd thought. "I sort of believe you."

"I could get used to hearing you say that."

The rolling *r*'s of the accent that caressed his perfect English thrummed that chord of ready desire that seemed to have come into existence in the core of her being. Instead of agitating her, it lulled her. She suddenly wanted to sleep. Like this. Ensconced in his power and protection.

She yawned. "You're comfy."

"*I* certainly am not comfy." His chuckle vibrated through her. But it was the powerful jerk against her buttocks, what she could no longer doubt was his hardness, seeming to be getting bigger, if that was possible, that lurched her out of her stupor.

He pulled her back against him. "Don't move."

"But you're...you're..."

"Aroused? Sure. I've been hard as steel since I laid eyes on you. And no, I'm not like that by default. But I don't mind."

"I thought men didn't mind anything more."

"I'm not 'men.' And even though it started out as uncomfortable, veered into painful and is now bordering on agonizing, I've never enjoyed anything more. I've never felt so alive."

She squirmed with his every word, only to be struck still when she realized it only made him harder. She'd never known mortification like this. Or arousal.

Her heart rattled her frame, until he pressed her closer to his body and whispered against her cheek, "I'll never do anything you don't invite me to, Talia. Beg me to."

She believed him. And she sagged back, savoring the way their bodies throbbed in unison. She'd probably be horrified later. But who cared about later when now was here? And like this?

She melted into him, felt her breathing and heartbeats match to his.

Endless minutes of shared tranquility and silent communion later, he kissed her forehead and sighed. "See that star? The one winking azure-blue? I'll call her Talia."

She nuzzled into his kiss, inviting a few more down her cheek, her core now so hot, so drenched and cramping she was breaths away from inviting more. Begging for it.

She pressed her thighs together, alleviating a measure of the pounding, and choked a thick murmur. "It must already have a name."

"I don't care. It reminds me of your eyes."

She giggled. "Maybe you should call it Talia's Eyes."

"Since it's only one, better yet Talia's Eye. So which will it be, *ya nadda jannati?* Talia's Left or Right Eye? I can foresee the myths that would one day be woven around such a name."

"Hmm, if I were a Cyclops, we wouldn't have this dilemma."

"If you were a Cyclops, they'd be the sexiest creatures to ever dominate men's fantasies."

She snorted. "And among all your skills, you acquired a black belt in far-fetched flirting?"

"You're right. I should have stuck with the truth. That it would dominate *this* man's fantasies. The two-eyed, sexy bundle of cuteness I'm wrapped around right now already does."

"I bet you wouldn't say that if you saw me in bloodstained scrubs with my hair spiked like a porcupine. Yeah, that 'atrocious' haircut wasn't for my disguise's sake. That's how I keep my hair out of my way and off my mind."

"You're talking to the man who found you overwhelmingly arousing when you were sporting a beard. I'd find you sexy if you were covered in mud. Oh, wait…now *there's* an idea."

"Mud-wrestling fantasies, huh? How mundanely male of you."

"I don't have those, no. But if it involves you and me, I'll definitely add them to my inventory of fantasies." She twisted around to glare up at him and he only whistled. "Whoa. Maybe I'll call it Talia's Glare."

"Since it's harsh and cold, huh?"

"Far from being either, this star, like your glare, is compelling, hypnotic, resolute, indomitable."

She almost did something stupid. Like kiss the aftertaste of those delicious words off his lips, or swirl her tongue in that solitary dimple that winked in his left cheek when he grinned.

She gave him a pseudo-self-important glance instead. "I'll have you know this glare has my interns and junior residents in the E.R. jumping and remaining in the air until I say down."

"I believe it." Suddenly he gathered her tighter. "Would you consider doing that here?"

Her heart veered in her chest. She struggled to spin

around further in his arms, came to lie sideways over him so she could more easily look into his eyes. "You mean work in an E.R. in Zohayd?"

"Actually, I'd love for you to consider training my men and women in field and emergency medicine."

"Oh…" The idea of remaining in Zohayd after they got through this, the fact that he esteemed her enough to offer her a responsibility like that, and elation at the thought of being where she could see him regularly erupted inside her.

Without thinking of the feasibility of such a scenario, she grinned up at him. "That sounds incredible!" It was only when his eyes blazed in return that she faltered. "I mean, we'll have to, y'know, talk this through when this is over…see if it's even plausible given why I'm here and all and—wait…women? You have *women* in your special forces?"

Impatience spurted in his eyes, probably since she'd changed the subject without giving him an answer. Then they softened again, perhaps in acknowledgment of the difficulties of their situation beyond the real and present danger. "Not many, since it doesn't seem to be one of the career options Zohaydan women prefer."

"I'm staggered that it *is* an option in Zohayd. That you have any."

His smile turned whimsical. "There *is* a difference between being a pigheaded, mulish ox and being a male chauvinist pig."

She rolled her eyes. "I'll never hear the end of that, will I?"

"Do you want to hear it?" he teased.

She thought for a moment. Then grinned impishly. "Nah."

With that, they both fell silent and snuggled deeper into each other as if by agreement.

After an hour of being melded together in deepening companionship, during which she'd simultaneously managed to remain molten and he to remain hard, they set off again.

The third day came. And passed.

At the end of the fourth day, their supplies had been all but exhausted. And there was no sign of the oasis.

On the fifth day, after sunset, as they'd set out on their cycle of hikes and rests, Harres had done something that had dread and desperation taking hold of her.

He'd dumped all their gear.

When she'd protested, he'd fallen silent for a long moment. Then he'd looked at her solemnly.

He'd said that she had no reason to believe he knew what he was doing anymore. But he could no longer afford to go at that pace. Would she trust him to know what they needed to survive, to reach the oasis?

And she'd trusted him.

But they hadn't reached the oasis.

Ten hours later, she'd been unable to go on.

She'd collapsed. Harres had managed to catch her before she hit the ground. He'd laid her down with utmost gentleness, held her in his solid embrace, raining on her soothing kisses and pleas for forgiveness.

She'd succumbed to unconsciousness thinking those would be the last things she felt and heard in her life.

But she woke up to find herself wrapped in the two blankets left with them. And Harres's jacket. She was parched and frying alive in the blistering heat of midday. Emphasis on *alive*.

And she realized another thing.

She was alone.

She struggled out of the tight cocoon, sat up. Harres was nowhere in sight.

He'd left her?

No. She knew he never would.

But what if something had happened to him? What if their enemies had found them? Would the prince of Zohayd be a bigger hand to gamble with in their quest for the throne? How would they use him? What would they do to him?

She sobbed. No tears came from her dehydrated eyes. She drifted in and out of consciousness. And even in waking moments, nightmares preyed on her. Showed her Harres, abused and worse, and all because he'd come for her....

Oh, God, Harres...please...

Then, as if in answer to her plea, he was there. She knew he wasn't *really* there. She was hallucinating with dehydration.

For this Harres was not the sand-car-and-helicopter-riding modern desert knight, but one on a white horse. Galloping her way as if he rode the wind, as one with the magnificent animal, made of the same energy, the same nobleness and fierceness and determination. Her knight coming to save her.

But there was no saving her. This was the end.

Not that it was too bad. She had only two regrets. That she hadn't saved Todd, and that she had let everything stand in the way between her and Harres.

If she had her time with him to live again, if she had more time with him, she would disregard it all and just be with him, experience all she could of him, while she could.

Now it was too late, and she would never know his passion for real.

What a waste.

Her dream Harres leaped off his horse before it came to a halt, spraying sand in a wide arc with the sudden abortion of its manic momentum. Harres descended on her, the wings of his white shroud spread like a great eagle's, enveloping her in peace and contentment. She was so thankful her intense desire had given her such a tangible last manifestation of the man she loved...yes, *loved*....

She could barely whisper her bliss to the apparition. "Harres...you feel so good..."

"Talia, *nadda jannati*, forgive me for leaving you."

"S'okay...I just wish...you didn't have...to leave, too."

His regal head, covered in a sun-reflecting white *ghotrah*, descended to protect her from the glare, his magical eyes emitting rays of pure-gold anxiety.

She sighed again. "You make...an incredible...angel, Harres. My guardian angel. Too bad you're here now...as that other angel guy...the death guy..."

"What?"

Talia winced. She'd been floating in the layers of Harres's voice, so deliciously deep and emotional. Now it boomed with sharpness and alarm.

"You're alive and you'll be well. Just drink, *ya talyeti*." She found nectar on her lips, gulped it without will or question, felt life surging into her as she sank in the delight of his crooning praise and encouragement to her, pouring hoarse explanations. "If I'd carried you, I wouldn't have been able to reach the oasis. So I left you, ran there. It took me six more hours, and two to ride back. I died of dread each second away from you. But I'm back, and you're alive, Talia."

"Y-you're sure?"

His face convulsed in her wavering focus. "Sure I'm sure. Now please drink, my precious dew droplet. Soon you'll be as good as ever."

"Don't you mean a-as bad?"

She felt herself gathered into arms that trembled, pressed against a chest that heaved, her depletion probably shaking up her perceptions. "There you are. My snarky gift from *Ullah*."

"You say…the most wonderful things. You are the most w-wonderful thing…that ever happened…to me…"

Then she surrendered to oblivion in the safety of his arms.

In the dreamscape that claimed her at once, she thought she heard him say, "It's you who are the most wonderful thing that ever happened to me, *ya habibati*."

Eight

Harres ignored pain, smothered exhaustion.

He had to last until he got Talia back to the oasis.

Those who'd ridden with him offered again to take care of her, of both of them.

He couldn't let them. Wouldn't. He had to be the one to carry her to safety. As he'd promised.

He asked a few of them to go back in his and Talia's tracks before they were wiped away by the incoming sandstorm, to retrieve what he'd ditched. The medical supplies most of all. He let those who stayed with him help secure Talia astride the horse, ensconced in his arms like he'd had her during their rests between the punishing hikes.

The ride back to the oasis took longer. Too long. Each moment seemed to expand, to refuse to let the next replace it, bound on prolonging his ordeal, on giving him more time to relive the hell of being forced to leave her behind.

He'd gone further out of his mind with each bounding

step away from her. He'd struggled to force himself to focus so he could see his path to the oasis, their ticket to survival. But the sight of her bundled up in blankets and ensconced in the barricade of a steep dune had been branded on his brain. He'd lost chunks of sanity with each hour, knowing the blankets' protection would turn to suffocation once the desert turned from an arctic wasteland to a blazing inferno. He'd prayed the message he'd left her in the sand wouldn't be wiped away by the ruthless winds, that she'd heard his plea before he'd left, to please, please wake up soon, read it, unwrap herself and use the blankets as shelter with the tent prop he'd kept.

But the message had been obliterated. And she'd unwrapped herself but hadn't taken refuge from the baking sun. After more than five days of ordeals almost beyond human tolerance, it had been a miracle she'd lasted that long. The only reason he had was because he was bound on saving her.

He gathered her tighter to his body, his heart draining of blood all over again as he imagined her waking up alone and finding no explanation for his disappearance.

It had been his miscalculations that had led to this situation. The terrain had changed beyond recognition from the last time he'd been there, and fearing the lethality of the quicksand areas that were the major factor behind the segregation of the oasis, he'd taken a much wider safety margin around their now obscured boundaries. He'd ditched their supplies too late, when doing so no longer meant quickening their progress, with irreversible exhaustion setting in.

He'd stumbled into the oasis's outer limits a few stages beyond depleted. He'd seen how he'd looked in the horrified expressions of those who'd run to him with water and efforts to spare him another step. Their horror had only risen when they'd realized he was bleeding. In his mad dash, he'd torn Talia's meticulous sutures.

He'd let the oasis people bandage and clothe him in weather-appropriate clothes, gulped down reviving drinks only because he knew he'd be no good to Talia if he didn't get repaired and refueled. He'd still given it all only minutes before he'd jumped on their most powerful endurance horse and exploded out of the oasis with their best riders struggling to keep up with him.

It had been another eternity until he'd gotten back to her.

He groaned. Even in the face of death, his Talia had been the essence of composure and grace. And wit. A chuckle sliced through him as her words echoed inside him again. Until he replayed her last ones before she'd surrendered to oblivion in his arms.

You are the most wonderful thing that ever happened to me….

He shuddered, pressed her closer as if to absorb her into him, where he'd always protect her with his very life.

She might have meant those words for her savior. But he'd reciprocated them, had meant them, for her.

After one more interminable hour, he brought his horse to a stumbling stop at the door of the cottage that had been prepared for them.

He only let others support Talia's weight for the moment it took him to sway off the horse. Then he reclaimed her, folded her into him as if he feared she'd evaporate if he loosened his hold.

Once inside the dwelling that he couldn't register beyond it being a roof over their head and a door cutting them off from the rest of the oasis, he coaxed the mostly unconscious Talia to drink again, glassfuls of both water and a high-calorie, vitamin and mineral drink the locals had concocted for conditions of extreme dehydration and sunstroke.

With utmost care, crooning encouragement and praise, he undressed her down to those ridiculous men's underwear, bathed her in cool water, fanned her dry and then sponged her down again, cooling her raging heat. When he finally judged her temperature within normal, he dressed her in one of the crisply clean, vibrantly colorful nightdresses the oasis women had provided.

Throughout, though her consciousness rose and fell like waves in a tranquil sea, she surrendered to his ministrations, unquestioning, unresisting.

He finally laid her down on the soft *kettan* linen sheets freshly spread on a firm mattress on top of a wide, low platform bed. As he withdrew, a distressed sound spilled from her suddenly working lips, her brow knotting as if in pain.

She couldn't bear separation from him. As he couldn't from her.

He came down beside her, cocooned her with his body. She burrowed deeper into him with each ragged breath until he felt she'd slid between the layers of his being, making him realize again that he'd had so many vacant places inside of him, ones she'd exposed. Ones only she could fill.

He stilled, savoring the imprint of each inch of her, vibrating to her every tremor, his rumbles harmonizing with her unintelligible purrs of fatigue and pure contentment.

Then she went limp and silent, her breath steadying, indicating her descent into replenishing sleep.

But he couldn't take that for granted.

At the tattered periphery of his awareness he thought he should seek the oasis elder and ask if there was still time before the sandstorm to have envoys sent to his brothers. Maybe if they moved fast enough, they'd get ahead of it.

But he couldn't bring himself to leave Talia. His only concern was to see to her health and comfort. Until she opened her eyes and her beloved personality shone at him through her heavenly gaze, he could think of nothing but her. Even the fate of Zohayd came second.

He'd do nothing but watch over her until she woke up....

Talia woke up.

For long moments after her eyelids scraped back over grit, she couldn't credit the images falling on her retinas.

She was ensconced in gossamer off-whiteness, drenched nerve-tingling spiciness and sourceless light.

Her surroundings came into sharper focus. She was actually surrounded by a fine mosquito net, lying in a gigantic bed on the smoothest linens she'd ever touched. She'd smelled the scents more than once since she'd come to Zohayd, seemingly a lifetime ago, incense of musk and amber and *ood*. The light was seeping from openings below a low ceiling blocked by arabesque work so delicate it must be almost as effective as the net.

She hadn't turned her head yet. She couldn't. But she saw enough to fascinate her on the side she could see. A wall of whitewashed mud-brick, a palm-wood door and window with shutters, cobblestone floors, two reed couches spread with wool cushions handwoven in a conflagration of color and pattern, with the same distinct Bedouin design gracing a rug and wall hangings. Oil lamps and incense burners hung on the wall, made of hand-worked bronze, simple, exquisite and polished to a dazzling sheen.

Was this another world? Another era?

She should know where she was. The knowledge just evaded her. She also knew she'd woken up many times before. If she could call the hazy episodes waking up. Now fragments of recollection clinked and bounced around like a rain of beads on the ground of her awareness.

Then as moments of wakefulness accumulated, the jittery particles settled, coalesced, stringing together to form a timeline. And she realized what had happened.

Harres had come back for her. Her desert knight had ridden back on a white horse, leading the cavalry. But not before she'd compounded dehydration and heat prostration with sunstroke.

No wonder distortions and abridgments stuffed her head. Yet one thing possessed hyperreality in the jigsaw of the haziness. Harres. Caring for and healing her. Looking so worn-out, so anxious, she would have wept had she been able to.

"Are you awake for real this time, *ya habibati?*"

His voice was as dark and haggard as she remembered from her delirium.

She twisted around, homing in on it. She found him two feet away on her other side, sitting on the floor with one knee bent, primed, slightly above her level with being so tall and her bed so low. He was wearing a white *abaya*.

So she hadn't imagined it.

She closed her eyes to savor the sight of him in his land's traditional garb. He looked regal in anything, but in this, he looked…*whoa*.

Yeah. *Whoa* should become a sanctioned adjective to describe the indescribable. Him. The ultimate in mind-blowing virility. Especially adorned in what he was born to wear.

He stood in one of those fluid moves that never ceased to amaze her, considering his size and bulk. Before her eyes could travel up to his, he swept the net surrounding her away and his *abaya* fell open.

Her gaze snagged on his chest. But for his bandages it was bare, a bronzed expanse of perfection and potency.

This was where she'd sought refuge from jeopardy and exhaustion, the haven that had turned their nightmare into a dream she'd cherish for the rest of her life.

His bandages were now narrower than she'd made them, exposing more of the ebony silk that accentuated each slope and bulge of sheer maleness. If that wasn't bad enough—or good enough—the tantalizing layer arrowed down over an abdomen hewn from living granite, guiding her eyes to where it began to flare…before it disappeared beneath string-tied white pants straight out of *Arabian Nights*. Those hung low, dangerously so, on those muscled hips, their looseness doing nothing to hide the power, the shape and size of his formidable thighs and manhood.

She couldn't breathe. Her insides contracted with a blow of longing so hard, she moaned with it.

Which was good news. If she could go from zero to one thousand in seconds at the mere sight of him, all her systems were functioning at optimum.

"Don't, *ya talyeti*. I beg you, don't close your eyes again."

She hadn't realized she'd squeezed them shut. His ragged plea and the dipping of the mattress jerked them open and up to his. And she moaned again.

The urgency in his eyes, in his pose, doused the heat spiraling through her. Even though his expression made him look more imposing, intimidating even, and even more arousing….

Enough. Say something!

She tried. Her throat was sore and as dry as the desert from disuse and the aftereffects of dehydration and exhaustion.

Her voice finally worked in a thready whisper. "I'm a-awake. For r-real."

He loomed over her, his eyes singeing her with the intensity of his examination and skepticism. "You said that before. Too many times. My sanity can't take much more false hope." He looked heavenward, stabbed his fingers through his hair. "What am I saying? If you're still sleep-talking, this won't make you snap out of it."

She struggled to sit up, managing only to turn fully toward him. "I a-am awake this time. I sort o-of remember the false starts. But I'm not only awake, I feel as good as new." His eyes darkened. "No, really. I've self-diagnosed since coming around, and I'm back to normal. I'm just woozy, which is to be expected, and sore from the exercise of my life and lying in bed too long…."

Her words petered out as she tried to sit up again and took her first look down her body.

She was in a low-cut, sleeveless satin nightdress in dazzling blues and greens and oranges, echoing the exuberance of the room's furnishings.

Heat rose as she imagined him taking her out of her clothes and dressing her in it. Her imaginings scorched her as they veered into vivid, languorous enactment of him taking her out of it again….

To make it worse, he was coming nearer, his anxiousness to ascertain her claim trapping her breath into suddenly full lungs, making the nightdress feel as if it had come alive, sliding over her nipples, slithering between her legs with knowing, tormenting skims, intensifying the heavy throb within.

She wriggled, trying to relieve her stinging breasts, squeezed her legs together to contain the ache building between them. She looked up at him with eyes barely open with the weight of desire. "Say…h-how long have I been out?"

He snapped a look at his watch, before looking back at her, his eyes losing their bleak look. "Fifty hours, forty-two minutes."

"Whoa!" she exclaimed, her voice regaining power and clarity with each syllable. "But that's a very acceptable time frame to get over a combo of dehydration and sunstroke. Good thing I'm a tough nut, eh?"

Elation dawned in his eyes, intensifying their vividness and beauty. "That you are, along with being an in-evaporable dew droplet. And *shokrun lel'lah*—thank God into infinity for that."

Her lips managed a tremulous smile. "So what have you been doing while I was sleep-talking?"

His lips quirked, the old devilry she knew and adored reigniting his eyes. "I took care of you, sent envoys out to my brothers, took more care of you. Then, oh, I took care of you."

She slapped his forearm playfully in response to his teasing then patted it in thanks for his effort to paint his grim vigil in lightness. "Did you take care of *you* at all? Did you get any sleep?"

He gave her a delicious look of mock contrition. "Not intentionally, I assure you."

She now saw the strain and exhaustion traversing his face in lines that hadn't been there even during their worst times. Her heart compressed even as it poured out a surplus of gratitude and admiration. "Oh, Harres, you're such an intractable protector." She caressed his forearm, basking in mixing their smiles. Then she gasped. "What about your wound? Did you get someone to look at it? How is it?"

He gave a perfect impression of a boy mollifying his

teacher before he revealed something that would send her screaming. "Uh—I have good news and bad news."

Her eyes flew over him, feverishly assessing his condition. No. Whatever his news was, it couldn't be terrible. Apart from the evident fatigue, he looked fine.

Her heart still quivered in her chest as she said, "Hit me with the bad."

He gave a pseudograve look. "Your sutures were very good."

"Past tense?" she squeaked. "You busted them!"

He nodded, holding his hands up. "Good news is, there's no sign of infection. See?" He moved his left arm up with minimal effort and no apparent discomfort. "What's more, the oasis people retrieved our medical kit, so you can sew me up again."

"You bet I will!" She subsided in relief at the proof that he was okay. Her eyes darted away from him for the first time and took in the whole room. She could see the rest of the place through the open door behind him. "This place is incredible."

"It is a very special place," he agreed. "It was the previous oasis-elder's dwelling. He died two years ago. Elders' houses remain uninhabited, as a tribute to their lives and leadership. It is an honor to be given this place during our stay."

Her smile trembled again. "Only the best for Zohayd's Guardian Prince."

He shook his head, his eyes bathing her in warmth. "It's not that. Any refugees they claimed back from the desert would have been given the same treatment. I also have a relationship with the people here that has nothing to do with me being their prince. I'm not sure they consider the Aal Shalaans their ruling family, or if they do, that they give the fact much significance."

"Why not?"

"The oasis and its people are considered off-limits to the outside world they live independent of. They are…revered by the rest of Zohayd and all the region, almost feared as a mystic nation who will always exist outside others' time and dominion."

She digested this, the feeling of being in another world and time intensifying, validated. "A nation? How many are they?"

"Around thirty thousand. Yet their refusal to join the modern world in any way makes them unique. Uniqueness is power beyond any secured by numbers."

"Not if they lack the modern methods of defending themselves against intruders, it isn't."

His face closed. "There will never be intruders. Not on the Aal Shalaans' watch. Not on mine."

She believed him. Harres the knight whose honor dictated he protect the helpless against the bullies of the world.

Suddenly, she felt she'd suffocate if she didn't feel him against her.

She held out trembling arms. "So, do I get a welcome back to the land of the awake?"

His face clenched with what looked like pain. For a heart-bursting moment, she feared he'd been placating her about his wound. Then his eyes filled with such turmoil, she thought she'd imposed on him.

Just before mortification caused her arms to slump to her sides, he groaned and sank into them.

The enormity of the reprieve, after thinking she'd lost her chance of having him like that, of everything, had her hands quaking as they slid over the breadth of his back, the leashed power of his arms. Her fingers caressed his vitality, his reality, committed every detail of him to tactile memory, felt him being integrated into her perceptions and senses.

Then she reached his face and translated into awareness what she'd been looking at and not fully registering.

"You shaved."

He smiled into her nuzzling, letting her singe her lips with the pleasure of coasting them over his perfect smoothness. "It was the first thing I did the moment a blade and disposable water were available."

She rubbed her lips over the underside of his jaw. "You know…I've never seen you clean shaven. When I first saw your face in that bathroom, you were already sporting a mighty ten-o'clock shadow."

He rubbed his chin over her cheek, giving her further demonstration of his silkiness. "So you approve?"

"I far, far more than approve."

Her lips traveled up until they glided hesitantly over his, her tongue tentatively laving them in tiny licks, still disbelieving the reality of experiencing this, of their texture and taste.

A rumble poured into her mouth, lancing into her heart just as it spiked her arousal to pain with its unadulterated passion.

Then he broke away from her quaking arms.

She had no power to drag him back into them. And no right, if this wasn't where he wanted to be.

He sat up, severing their connection. Then he rose off the bed altogether.

He stood above her, his heavy-lidded eyes obscuring his expression for the first time since…ever.

Then he drew both hands through his hair and exhaled. "You might be awake, but you're not really all there yet. And you are—fragile, in every way." His shoulders rose and fell on another exhalation. "So now we get you back to fighting form."

Was that why he'd pulled back? He wanted her back to

full health, physically and mentally, before he'd consider changing their status quo?

It made sense. And made her even more grateful to him, if that was possible.

She was a cauldron of seething emotions and needs right now, had no control over any of them. And she needed to know if what she felt melting all resistance was the ordeal talking, the days of inseparable proximity and total dependence, or if the feelings originated from her.

Now that stress and danger were over, would the physical and emotional pull remain this overwhelming? Would he remain the same man who'd done everything to keep their spirits up? It had niggled that he might have exaggerated his attraction to her for many worthwhile ends. Survival, smoothing over a bumpy beginning. And maybe not so worthwhile ones. Gaining his objective—the secret to secure his family and their throne.

So many things hung like a sun-obliterating cloud over the whole situation. Todd's ordeal, the Aal Shalaans' role in it and their current danger, the info she'd stumbled on, Harres's duty as guardian of his family and people.

So he'd done the right thing by drawing away. She'd follow his lead, recover her health and clarity. Until she figured out what was real. Inside her, around her, about him, between them. Or until this mess, this assortment of *messes,* was sorted out.

If they possibly could be.

Nine

A string of eruptions reverberated in Talia's bones.

She would have taken instinctive cover if Harres's arm hadn't been around her shoulder.

He gave her a reassuring squeeze, chuckled in her ear. "No, that's not a firing squad."

Gulping down her heart, she let him resume leading her through the hurrying crowd, still not sure where their destination was, where the feast was being held. "A gun salute for the Guardian Prince of Zohayd, then?"

His grin widened. "That's just how they announce the beginning of their entertainment."

"With an aerial blitz?"

He threw his magnificent head back and laughed before looking his pleasure and merriment down on her. "The extra zeal is in honor of your recovery and your gracing of their feast tonight."

She raised him a wider grin, her heart zooming again

with elation, with anticipation. But mostly, with his nearness.

She'd been up and about for three days now, had recovered fully. But what relieved her was the condition of his wound. Her sutures had been very good. And had remained mostly intact, with only a few needing reapplication. The healing had been spectacular. She'd never known humans could heal that fast. She kept teasing that he must have mutants or local gods in his ancestry. Which wouldn't surprise her.

And during the idyll of recuperation and recreation, they'd remained in the cottage or its garden, with the oasis people coming periodically to check their needs and replenish their supplies. She hadn't wanted to go out, to see more.

She'd had Harres with her.

She now knew that the bonds of harmony and sufficiency they'd forged during their desert trek hadn't just been crisis induced. It hadn't been the isolation or the desperation. It all originated from their unpressured choices, their innate inclinations, their essential selves, and flowed between them in a closed circuit of synergy and affinity.

Being with him *was* enough. Felt like everything.

Tonight was the first night they would join the oasis people. She felt so grateful to them, so humbled by their hospitality. But earlier she'd felt embarrassed, too.

The oasis-elder's wife and daughters had come, bringing her an exceptionally intricate and stunningly vivacious outfit to wear to the feast. As Harres had stood beside her translating their felicity at her recovery and her thrill over their magnificent gift, the ladies had eaten him up with their eyes. She'd wanted to jump to their side and indulge in the pleasure of *oohing* and *aahing* over the wonders of him with those born equipped to appreciate them. Which was every female with a pulse.

But it had been when their eyes had turned to her with knowing tinged with envy that she'd realized. With her and Harres's living arrangement, they must think they were… intimate. And if she was truthful, and she was, they hadn't been only because of his consideration and restraint.

Not one to let misgivings go unvoiced, she'd asked. Was their situation compromising him, a prince in an ultra-conservative kingdom? Now that her staying with him was no longer necessary, couldn't she move elsewhere until his brothers came for them?

He'd said that the oasis people didn't follow any rules but their own. Being one with nature, living outside the reach of politics or material interests, they didn't police others' morality and conduct, lived and let live. But even if they hadn't, he cared nothing for what the world thought. He cared only about what she wanted. Did *she* want to move out?

Her heart thudded all over again at the memory. He'd been so intense, yet indulgent, not taking it for granted that she didn't want to. And she didn't. She couldn't even think how fast the day was approaching when she would move out of his orbit, return to a life that didn't have him in it.

She couldn't think, so she didn't. Plenty of time later to. Her lifetime's worth.

Now with her heart thudding, she investigated the external source of pounding.

In the dual illumination of a waxing moon and raging fires, she saw it was coming from the direction of the biggest construction she'd seen so far in the oasis.

Silvered by moonbeams and gilded by flickering flames, a one-story circular building rose among a huge clearing within the congregation of dwellings. It was made of the same materials but could accommodate probably a few thousand. It had more windows than walls, and flanking its single door, older women in long-sleeved flowing dresses with tattoos covering their temples and chins were squatting on the ground, each with a large wooden urn held between bent legs, pounding it with a two-foot pestle.

He smiled into her eyes. "When it's not used as a percussion instrument, the *mihbaj* doubles as a seed grinder, mainly coffee, and…" A storm of new drumming drowned out his voice, coming from inside the building, making him put his lips to her ears. "The whole rhythm section has joined in. Let's go in."

As they did, she felt as if she'd stepped centuries back into the ancient orient with its special brand of excesses.

The ambiance was overpowering in richness and depth and purity with an edge of mystic decadence to it. Heavy sweet-spicy *ood* incense blended with the distinctive smell of fruit-mixed tobacco that many smoked in their water-filled *sheeshas*. The fumes undulated like scented ghosts, twining through the warm, hypnotic light flickering from hundreds of polished, handcrafted copper lanterns.

The huge circle of the floor was covered in handwoven rugs, the whitewashed walls scattered in arabesque windows, most thrown open to let in the desert-night breeze and the rising moon rays.

All around, multitudes of exuberant cushions were laid on the floor and against the walls, with *tableyahs*—foot-high, unpolished wooden tables—set before them for the banquet.

On the unfurnished side, a three-foot-high platform hosted the dozens of drummers producing that blood-seething rhythm.

"The tambourine-like instrument is the *reg*. The *doff,* the large one with no jangles, acts as the bass drum." She followed Harres's pointing finger, eagerly imbibing the info. "But it's the *darabukkah,* the inverted vaselike drums, whose players keep up the hot rhythm. Usually they wow the crowd with some impossibly complex and long routines before the other instruments join in."

They sure wowed *her*. She felt the rhythm boiling her blood, seeping into her nervous pathways, taking hold of her impulses.

She let Harres guide her to the seating arrangement. But with every step she swayed more to the rhythm, her every cell feeling like popcorn, ricocheting inside her with the need to expend the surplus energy gathering in them in unbridled motion.

Suddenly Harres took her hand and spooled her away then back into his arms, all while moving as one with the beat. "Dance, *ya nadda jannati*. Celebrate being alive and being in paradise."

And being with you, she wanted to shout.

She didn't, let her eyes shout it for her. Then she danced, as if she'd been released from shackles that had kept her immobile all her life, riding the compelling rhythm, moving with him to the primal beat, her heart keeping the same fiery tempo.

Somehow, they wound up in the middle of a dancing circle that he'd either led her to or had formed around them.

The young tribe members swirled around them in intricate routines, the males swooping like birds of prey, bounding and stomping in energetic courtship and persistent demand, the females twirling around like huge flowers, gesturing and tapping in practiced coquetry and eager acceptance.

Harres led her in emulating them, then in improvising their own dance of intimacy and delight in each other.

And for an indeterminate stretch, she felt she'd been transported to another realm where nothing existed but him. She felt him, and only him, as his eyes and touch lured her, inflamed her, shared with her, joined with her, as he moved with her as if they were connected on all levels, as if the same impulses coursed in their nerves, the same drive powered their wills and limbs.

She surfaced from the magical realm to everyone singing. In moments she found herself repeating the distinctive, catchy melody and lyrics, without understanding a word.

Suddenly Harres pulled her to him, turning the energy of their dance into a slow burn of seduction, his lips at her ear shooting more bolts of stimulation through her. And that was before she heard what he whispered.

"Everything before you passed and went to waste."

Her whole frame jerked with the shock, the emotions that surged too fast, too vast to comprehend, to contain.

He pressed her nearer, his voice deeper, darker, the only thing she heard anymore. *"Koll shai gablek addaw daa."*

That was what she was singing along.

Harres was just translating.

But no. He wasn't. He meant it. Even if the magic of those moments, of their situation and surroundings was amplifying his emotions…

The music came to an abrupt end. The silence that exploded in the next moment felt like a freezing splash, dousing her fire.

No. She wanted this time out of time to continue, to last.

But she knew it wouldn't. None of it would.

She could only cherish every second, waste none on despondency.

She looked up at Harres, found him looking back at her with eyes still storming with stimulation. She teetered from his intensity, from the drain of energy. He bent and lifted her into his arms.

People ran ahead, indicating the place of honor they should occupy. She tried to regain her footing, but he only tightened his hold on her. She struggled not to bury her face in his shoulder in embarrassment, to be carried like that, and after the whole tribe saw her dancing like a demon, too.

At their place, he set her on the cushions, sat down beside her and fetched her water and *maward*—rose essence. Then he began peeling ripened dates and feeding them to her.

She fought the urge to do something to be really embarrassed about. Grabbing his hand and suckling the sticky sweetness off his fingers. Then traveling downward…

Going lightheaded with the fantasies, with holding back, she mumbled around the last mouthful, "You do know I'm fully recharged and in no need of coddling, right?"

He shook his head. "You used up your battery with that marathon jig."

She waved her hand. "I'm just saving up for the next one."

He smiled down at her, poured her some mouthwatering cardamom coffee in a tiny, handblown, greenish glass and brought it to her lips. "A sip with each bite of dates is the recommended dose."

She did as instructed, her eyes snapping wider at the incredible blend of aromas and flavors, of bitterness and sweetness, at the graininess of the dates dissolving in the rich heat and smoothness of the coffee.

She sighed, gulped the rest. Sinking deeper in contentment, she turned to adjust her cushions. He jumped to do it himself.

She leaned back on them, quirking her lips at him. "When will you believe you don't have to keep doing stuff for me, that I've never been in better shape? No emergency doctor could have done a better job on me."

"I know, my invincible dew droplet, but would you be so cruel as to deprive me of the pleasure of pampering you?"

Now what could a woman say to *that?*

Nothing but unintelligible sighs, evidently. That was all that issued from her as the oasis elder rose to deliver a word of welcome before waiters with huge trays holding dozens of plates streamed out to serve dinner.

More sighs accompanied the fantastic meal. The food at the oasis was the best she'd ever had. Tonight it rose to ambrosia level.

Harres fed her, cut the assortment of grilled meats, told her the names and recipes of the baked and grilled breads and the vegetable stews. He introduced her to date wine, which she proclaimed should replace nectar as the drink of the gods. But it was *logmet al gadee* that was truly out of this world. The golden spheres of fried dough, crunchy on the outside, soft on the inside and dipped in thick syrup were so good there should be—and probably there was—a penalty for it.

After dinner they danced again, then she shook hands with hundreds of people, thanked them all for the best night of her life. On their stroll back to the cottage, she decided something.

Everything in this place was pure magic.

But she knew that wasn't an accurate assessment. Had she been with anyone else, she wouldn't have enjoyed it a fraction as much. She'd been to idyllic places for vacations before, but had never enjoyed one after her parents died, had stopped trying to years ago....

"What are you thinking, *ya talyeti?*"

She shook off the surge of melancholy, smiled up at him. "This means my Talia, right?"

He nodded, sweeping a soothing hand over her hair, now

supple and sparkling from a miraculous blend of local oils. "Your Arabic is getting better every day."

"I find it fascinating, so rich and expressive in ways so different from English. I'd love to learn more."

"Then you shall."

It was always like that. She wished for something, and he insisted she'd have it. She knew he *would* give her anything, if at all possible.

Feeling her skin getting tighter with emotion, she answered his previous question. "I was thinking of my parents."

His eyes grew softer. "You told me they died. I didn't want to probe. Not a good idea bringing up death and that of loved ones in our situation back then."

"But you want to know now."

"Only if it doesn't pain you to talk about them."

"No, no. I love to talk about them. I hate it that people avoid bringing them up, as if it will remind me of their loss. As if I need to be reminded. It's actually not mentioning them that makes me feel their absence even more acutely."

His eyebrows knotted. "People can be misguided in their good intentions." His brow cleared, his lips quirking. "What I find amazing is that you didn't set them straight."

"Oh, I did."

He chuckled before gentle seriousness descended over his face. "Were their deaths recent?"

"It *feels* like yesterday. And like a few lifetimes ago."

"I know what you mean."

Her heart kicked. "You've lost loved ones, too?"

He shook his head, his gaze heating. "I meant knowing you. It's so vivid it feels perpetually new, yet so powerful it feels as if you have been there all my life, a part of my being." Now what could she say to something so—indescribable?

And worse, that sounded so spontaneous and sincere? Good thing he didn't let her struggle for a comment, but went on. "But I don't have a comparable experience when it comes to losing someone that dear. My mother died when I was five, so I hardly remember her. So tell me, *ya talyeti,* talk to me about your loved ones."

"I feel I lost them simultaneously, even though they died seven years apart. Okay, let me start at the beginning." She let out a shuddering exhalation, let him draw her closer into him, then began. "I never knew my biological father. I knew *of* him, but he didn't want a wife and a kid, let alone two. We had our mother's family name until she married the man I consider my father when Todd and I were two. As I grew up and learned the whole story, I thought my mother the luckiest woman on earth and my father—the man whose name I carry now—the best man in existence. I never saw anyone more in love or right for each other than they were.

"The only problem was, my father was almost thirty years older than my mom. He'd never been married before, always said he'd been waiting for her. For all of us. When I was in my second year in med school, right before his eightieth birthday, he passed away in his sleep, beside my mom. She never recovered. Seven years later, she overdosed on a concoction of the prescription meds I'd been begging her for years not to take. I could have saved her if I was there, but only Todd was home. By the time the ambulance arrived, it was too late."

For long moments after she fell silent, Harres said nothing. Then they entered their cottage, and he pulled her into his embrace, pressed her head against his endless chest.

They stood like that, sharing, savoring, her body throbbing to the tempo of the powerful heart beating below her ear.

Then he kissed the top of her head. "*Ana aassef, ya nadda jannati.* I'm sorry."

He said nothing more. Then they went about their bedtime routine. Once in bed, hearing him moving in the other room, she had a sudden realization. Why she'd always given up on any attempt at a relationship so early, so easily.

With her parents' example, she'd set her own bar high. Every connection she'd attempted had fallen miles below it. She'd soon given up on trying, had been resigned that she'd never have anything like they'd had, and that if she couldn't, she'd rather be alone. She'd become content with a life full of activity and purpose.

Now there was Harres.

"It's…huge."

At Talia's exclamation, Harres pressed his hard body to her back, murmured in her ear, "Yes, it is."

She nestled back against him, cast her gaze over the depression of *el waha*—the oasis that sprawled below them.

It had taken the past four days to cover the place on horseback. Now, on top of Reeh—or Wind, the white horse Harres had ridden on his charge back to save her—she had the best vantage point yet to appreciate it all from.

It seemed the explosion of life among the barrenness of the desert fed the conditions that fueled its proliferation in an endless cycle of balance and symbiosis. Date palms and olive trees numbered in the hundreds of thousands. Wildflowers and cacti were impossible in beauty and abundance. Farmed fruits and vegetables, especially figs, apricots, berries and corn, were astounding in size and taste. And besides horses, camels, sheep, goats, cats and dogs, there were innumerable representatives of the animal kingdom, all like the residents, unstressed and unthreatened.

Deer and foxes let her walk up to them, a few let her pet them. Even reptiles and birds humored her when she cooed to them and presumed to offer them food and seek their acquaintance.

She sighed her pleasure again. "Scratch huge. It's endless. It goes on forever."

Harres chuckled as he unwrapped her from his arms, jumped off the horse and reached up to carry her down. His effortless strength and the cherishing in his glance and touch as she slid down his body sent a current through her heart.

"We can see about three miles to the horizon if we're on the ground, farther the higher up we go. Since we're three hundred feet up, we can see for about twenty miles. And since the oasis measures more than that on its narrowest side, you can't see its end from any point, making it look endless."

She whooped, loving his explanations. "You should consider a career as a tour guide, if ever princes are no longer in demand…." She bit her tongue. Not something to joke about with a dethroning conspiracy going on in his kingdom. He only grinned at her, showing her he knew she'd meant nothing, enjoyed her joke. Grinning back in relief, she said, "I can now see how this place earned its mystical reputation."

"So it's worth the ordeal I put you through coming here, eh?"

"I would have welcomed a trash dump if it had water and shelter. But it isn't because this place meant life to us that I find it amazing. It is a paradise, like you said. Mostly because of its inhabitants. Everyone is so kind and bright and wise."

She left out the main reason why she found this place enchanting. The present company.

For minutes, as sunset expanded its dominion over the oasis, boosting the beauty to its most mind-boggling, he guided her to a spring of crystalline water enclosed within a canopy of palms. The air was laden with sweet plant scents and heady earth aromas, its temperature seeming to be calibrated for perfect comfort, all year round as he'd told her.

As they stopped by the spring, she said, "It would be so easy to live here forever."

If Todd was with her, she amended inwardly, or at least out of prison.

Harres spread a rug at her feet, looked up. "Wouldn't you go out of your mind without modern conveniences?"

She sank down on the rug, reached for their food basket. "Sure, I'd miss a few things. Hot showers for one. And the internet. Uh...I'm sure there's more I'd miss, but I'm drawing a blank right now."

He got out glasses. "How about medicine?"

"Oh, I'd practice it here like I have been so far. I'd probably do far more good in the long run than I do patching up people who go out and drive recklessly or OD again."

He raised a slice of apricot to her lips. "But you're a very complex being, *ya nadda jannati,* a product of dozens of centuries of human evolution. I am best qualified to judge how sturdy and tenacious you are, but beyond the comforts you'd substitute with the pleasures of healthy living and labor, you'd itch for what the people here can't conceive, need challenges they can't provide."

He knew her too well. And she could say the exact same of him. She nodded. "Probably. It's just the simplicity, the contentment and tranquility that breathes in this place is enchanting. If I had my way, this would be normal life and the bustle of the twenty-first century would be the vacation."

"Then you will have your way."

It felt like a pledge. As if he never meant this to end.

Yet she had no illusions, no hopes. Oceans of harsh realities, mountains of obstacles existed between them.

She was a commoner from another country and culture and he was a prince with a binding duty to his people. Then there was Todd's ordeal. She had no idea what securing his freedom would mean, to Harres, to his family. Even if there could be a solution that didn't end up harming them and making her Harres's enemy, he was probably—like that woman her brother had fallen in love with—intended to marry for king and kingdom.

Not that she'd ever put Harres and marriage together in a linear thought where *she* was concerned.

She now watched as he braided palm leaves into an ingenious basket for her fruits. Then she said, "You know, I came here thinking all of you Aal Shalaans were pampered perverts, mired in excess, useless at best, and helpless without your guards and gadgets, that all there was to you was unearned wealth and inherited status."

His nimble hands had stopped midway through weaving his own basket, his eyes becoming somber, contemplative. Then he inhaled. "So what did you think of me specifically?"

She owed him the truth, no matter how ugly it was. Feeling shame surge into her cheeks, she said, "When I first heard the tales of your valor and victories? I thought you were the most obnoxious of the lot, playing at being a hero, taking credit for the achievements of the true but faceless heroes, or at best relying on the safety net of your men's lives and your endless resources to play the role of Zohayd's Guardian Prince. I thought you'd show your true colors when you were stripped of your force field of assets."

He put a palm over his heart. "Ouch. And now you

think all that plus a few more choice put-downs and denigrations?"

She cast him a reproachful glance. "You know what I think now."

"Tell me."

The way he'd said that. The way he looked at her. As if he couldn't live without this vital knowledge.

Breath left her. "You know what you are. You have a whole kingdom who revere the dirt beneath your feet."

He sat up slowly. "Reverence doesn't matter to me. I never do anything in anticipation of anyone's thanks or admiration. I surely don't expect either, or care if I get them."

Her lips twitched. "Too bad. You'll just have to keep your chin up and take shiploads of both like the worshipped prince you are. Judging by the way the oasis inhabitants treat you, you're far more than that to them. And it *is* only you, not the whole royal family. You personally have done so much for them."

"I only do what I am in a position to do. I don't deserve credit or gratitude for doing my duty, but I would have earned disrespect and disrepute if I didn't."

"As you say around here, 'squeeze a lemon on it,'" she teased.

"So I can stomach the queasiness of adulation? Do you at least believe I never expect, let alone crave, any of it?"

"Oh, yes. I saw you squirming when they told tales of your glories last night. You sure don't crave anyone's adulation."

"I didn't say *that*."

Her heart punched her ribs. "You...crave mine?"

His nod was solemn. "I crave your acceptance, your approval."

"Uh…you have been around the past two weeks, right?"

He rose until he was on his knees, towering over her. "I need to hear it, *ya nadda jannati,* in your inimitable words. What you think of me is the only validation I have ever craved."

She struggled with an attack of arrhythmia. But he'd demanded. And the truth was his due, the least she could give him when she owed him her very life.

She gave it to him. "From the first moment, you forced me to reassess you. With every action and word, you showed me you are all that's advertised and far more. Stripped from all the trappings of your power, you proved to be the total opposite of what I thought, with stamina and resourcefulness and bravery that constantly awe me. You showed me you take your duty to protect anyone weaker than you, at whatever cost to you, more seriously than I thought possible in this day and age. I believe you're one of a kind, Prince Harres Aal Shalaan."

His gaze lengthened, heated, until she felt she'd burst into flames. Just when she was about to whimper, *please, enough,* he took her hand, buried his face in its palm for a long moment.

Then raggedly, still against her flesh, he whispered, "You honor me with your opinion. I will always strive to deserve it."

From then on, the atmosphere seemed charged with emotion, intensifying each sensation into near distress.

As if by agreement, they barely spoke as they had their meal. She was thankful for the silence. It gave her the chance to deal with her upheaval and face herself with more truths.

There were Aal Shalaans who hadn't hesitated to destroy Todd's life to gain their ends, but she could no longer dip the whole family in the bile of her anger and prejudice. And just as she didn't know who exactly among the Aal Shalaans and Ghada's family were culpable, there could be sides to the story that would change her perspective. Whatever *that* became, she now believed, from Harres's example, that the Aal Shalaans weren't an evil regime that deserved to be deposed.

Which led her to more realizations. And a decision.

Soon it got chilly and they rode through the now sleeping oasis back to the cottage under the blaze of a full moon.

Inside, they took turns bathing.

The moment he came out into the sitting area, she began. "I decided something when I thought I was dying."

His smile froze, his face slamming shut. "Don't say that again. Don't even think it."

"I need to tell you this." She waited until he gave a difficult nod, then went on. "When I thought it was over, I thought that if I had a chance to do things over, or a second chance to put things right, I'd do what I really wanted to do, with no thought to obstacles or misgivings or consequences. Then you saved me. And I got cold feet."

He didn't ask her to elaborate. He just stared at her, seriousness seizing his face fully for the first time.

She knew this would lead nowhere. And it made no difference.

She loved him. A love that permeated her soul and traversed her being. A love forged in shared danger, fortified by the certainty of mutual reliance. And she was no longer letting anything stop her from expressing that love, from taking what she could with him, of him.

She rose from the low couch, her steps impeded by the ferocity of her emotions. She stopped before him, looked up into the eyes that meant everything to her. Then she made the leap.

"You told me you'd never do anything I didn't want you to, didn't beg you to do. So here I am, begging you. I want you, Harres. I want nothing but you."

Ten

So this was temptation.

Unstoppable, irresistible. To die for.

This golden virago who'd invaded his being, occupied his mind and heart, conquered his reason and priorities.

She stood before him, open, offering everything. He could feel, in every nuance of his essence, the totality of her offer. It wasn't only of her body and pleasures. She was bestowing all she had, all she was, on him.

And if he closed the gap between them now, he'd take all of her, consume her.

But how could he when he couldn't give his all in return?

She *did* have all of him, Harres, the man, the human being. She had since that first night in the desert, when they'd been stripped to their essentials, when their souls had mingled in the most profound ways possible. If he'd had any concerns that the ordeal had augmented his feelings, influenced their depth and direction, the past ten days had erased them, had replaced them with certainty and wonder.

Added to how she'd awed him with the way she'd handled their trials, stood up to and beside him. She'd delighted him with every second of their stay in the oasis. After only a week, even with the language obstacle, she was already the more favorite among the inhabitants.

The day after the feast, she'd set up a clinic, offered her services. He'd thought those who'd relied on healing practices passed down through generations would shy away from her and her modern medical practices and instruments. But she'd anticipated that, offered only her medical skills and whatever the oasis provided of supplies and medicines. After a slow day, she'd been called to an obstructed labor, where she'd saved both mother and twin babies.

Then she'd become a legend. People had flooded in. They'd stood in queues from morning till sunset, when he, who acted as her assistant, insisted the doctor needed rest. She kept proving how she, too, needed nothing beyond her diverse skills to survive and excel anywhere, under any conditions. He told her she was the epitome of the Arabic proverb "A skilled woman weaves with a donkey's leg" and teased her about being Dr. MacGyver.

She wasn't just a healer, but a warrior and a protector like him. She shared his soul in all its breadth and peculiarities. He wanted, *needed* to share the rest of himself with her, for the rest of his life. There was no doubt in him anymore. Harres, the man, was hers. Forever.

And though Harres the prince had divided loyalties, that wasn't what stopped him from proclaiming his love, his devotion. Only one thing did. Her grievance against his family. If everything she'd told him was the truth, she had legitimate reason to want to bring his family—which she perceived as a unit that worked to the same end of retaining power—to her brand of justice. What if he couldn't secure her brother's release and redemption? How could he take her, when he couldn't promise that in return?

Turmoil ripped the bindings of his heart. And that was before she closed her eyes, her chin trembling as two crystalline tears escaped her luxurious lashes.

Then she raised glistening azure eyes and he nearly had a heart attack. "I thought you wanted me, too...."

He couldn't bear it. *Elal jaheem* with the obstacles between them. He *would* obliterate them.

With a sob, she began to turn away. He grabbed her hand, placed it on his chest, felt as if his heart would ram through it to feel the touch of that hand that healed so many, that had saved him.

Her hand shook under his, each tremor an electric shock. Her words' effect was more brutal.

"Just forget I said anything. I've put you in an awkward position, what with all the things that remain unresolved. And then you've probably been flirting with me with no intention of taking it any further, and I understand your motivation, totally—"

"Oh, shut *up*."

Her mouth fell open at his growl, her eyes snapping wide, those eyes that glowed an unearthly blue in the vividness of the honey tan the desert sun had poured over her.

He looked down at her in that satiny dress that hung from her shoulders in relaxed pleats to the floor, another that the oasis women had given her in a shade that attempted to emulate the eyes that so fascinated them. The dress was by no stretch sexy. Not on anyone else. On her, it was the ultimate in eroticism.

She fidgeted, tried to escape his gaze. He wouldn't let her, his other hand capturing her delectable chin.

"Do I have your attention, *ya nadda jannati?*" He waited until she raised moist eyes to him and gave a hesitant nod. "First, yes, ultimately major issues are unresolved." She gasped, tried to wriggle out of his hold. He clung tighter, his hold growing gentler until she subsided in it, gave him her wounded gaze. He groaned. "But not where I'm concerned. My father once told me a man is granted one certainty in his life, one perfection. And it's up to him to recognize it, to seize it, to let it bless his life. He wasted his, for reasons that seemed imperative at the time. My younger brother Shaheen just found his certainty, and learning from our father's mistake, didn't let anything stop him from seizing it. I thought *my* certainty was that I'd never have such perfection. I lived at total peace with that. At least, I did until I found it. Found *you*. So no, Talia, I don't *want* you."

The eyes that had been misting with an escalation of emotion jerked with stricken confusion. Eyes to bring a man, willingly, eagerly, to his knees.

They brought him to his before her.

She gasped, swayed, then a hot sound of protest broke from her as she tried to pull him back up.

He only brought her hand to his lips and pledged it all to her. "*Ana ahebbek, aashagek ya talyeti, ya noor donyeti*—I love you, worship you, and more, my Talia, light of my world."

She went totally still. Her tremors stopped. Her breathing. Her stare emptied of all but shock.

Then she shook her head. "I—I don't—you don't have to say that…I just want to be with you while I can…so don't… don't…"

He rose, gliding his aching body against hers, catching her around her hips and raising her up until she was blinking her surprise down at him. His heart quivered at the incredible sight and feel of the treasure filling his arms, his lips spreading with the pleasure. "I am getting good at getting you to shut up and listen. And yes, *ya talyeti,* I do have to say this, because it's what I feel, *all* that I feel."

She wriggled in his arms until she made him put her down. He smiled all his love down at her, willing her to read into his heart. But when the flabbergasted look in her eyes, the distress didn't waver, uncertainty crept up on him.

Had he seen and felt more from her than there actually was? She wanted to act on the desire that had raged between them from the first moment, but that was all?

The unbearable doubt with all its ramifications hit him like a barrage of bullets in his gut. He swayed back under its brunt.

At last, he rasped the most difficult words he'd ever uttered in his life, "If you don't reciprocate, just walk away, and we'll forget *I* ever said anything."

With his certainty shattered, the expressions that wove in her eyes tangled in his mind. He stopped trying to analyze them, too afraid to hope, too scared she'd end hope.

"You won't take me up on my offer?" she said, slow and husky.

His heart contracted. "Not if you don't feel the same."

Suddenly, something he'd never thought to see in her eyes almost had him flat on his back. A look of unadulterated seduction, so hungry and demanding and erotic, he could swear he heard hormones roar in his arteries.

His arousal jerked painfully. And that was before she gave him a reason-numbing body rub with her hot firmness.

"Sure I can't change your mind about that?" she purred against his neck before sinking her teeth in his jaw.

"Talia…" He growled his agonized stimulation, his

whole body turning to rock with the need to crush her to him.

Before he could push away, her hands tangled in his hair and dragged his head down.

He knew if she kissed him, he wouldn't be able to stop. And he'd rather not have her at all than have her in every way but the one that mattered.

He turned his face away, felt her scorching lips latch on to his cheek, open, moist, devouring. "Don't…"

"Oh, shut *up*."

Her aggressive growl ended with a sharp tug on his hair. Then before his overcharged nerves could fire one more impulse, her lips sank onto his, paralyzing him with their hunger, with their softness and fragrance and taste.

Before the pain of it all could travel to his core, shatter it, she moaned inside him, "I thought it was impossible, but I can love you more. You just made me."

He jerked back, she clung. His whole system was going haywire from the mixed signals. He groaned. "You love me?"

She spread nips and nibbles over his jaw, detonating depth mines of pleasure and ferocity in his blood. "Down to your last pore. I'm sure I'd find even your cellular structure pant-worthy."

The image her words painted, their import, struck him. And just like that, everything inside him surged with jubilation.

He squeezed her off the ground, held her up high, guffawed. "Only you. Only you would say this, my unique dew droplet. I did have to go fall in love with a doctor."

She braced her hands on his shoulders, her eyes burning with desire dueling with challenge dipped in insecurity. "Of all the women you wade in, huh? I did hear the Guardian Prince was also the sultan of a worldwide harem."

He put her down, caught her face in an adamant grip. "Only one woman for me. Ever. You. And I would say everything before you went to waste, but it didn't. It did serve a great purpose. To make me recognize the certainty of your perfection for me faster, appreciate it with everything in me."

She only nodded, her eyes now inundating him with everything in her. She believed him. With just his word. And she was making him believe, too. That he had all of her.

He now truly had the whole world.

He bent, breathed her in, angled his lips against hers. Then he sank. He felt life rush through him, passion cresting in dark, overwhelming waves, crashing inside him. Magic. And love. More. Adoration and beyond. His Talia.

"Talyeti, enti elli, wana elek," he growled in her mouth, between tongue thrusts that breached the sweetness she surrendered with such mind-destroying eagerness. "You're mine. And I'm yours."

"Yes, yes…" She snatched at his lips, hers rising in heat. "How do I say 'my Harres'?"

"Harresi," he groaned.

"Harresi. My guardian knight."

And he did feel hers. Owned. And delirious to be so.

He sank to his knees before her again, bunched her dress in his fists, raised it up in inches, replacing it with his lips, tongue, teeth, coating her velvet firmness in suckles and bites, skimming and tantalizing her, lingering and tormenting himself. Her moans echoed his groans, became keens, then pants.

When he could no longer bear it either, he exploded up and took her dress with him. She flung up her supple arms in a sweep of eagerness and surrender, helping him, urging him. He snatched the garment away as if it was his worst enemy. But before he could step back and look on the treasure he'd uncovered, her hands were attacking his clothes with the same vehemence.

She tore the *abaya* off his shoulders and down his arms. Then with him still entangled in its tethers, she devoured him, her tongue painting him in ravenous greed, her teeth sinking into his flesh in delicate bites, each nip a new lash of arousal. He lurched under the power of each one. Then she moaned, "You taste and feel as magnificent as you look. I want more of you, all of you."

He roared. The pressure in his loins was becoming unbearable. He had to stop her, pull back from the precipice or this wouldn't be the languorous seduction he'd planned it to be. Any more and it would be like a dam breaking the moment he thrust inside her.

No. He wouldn't let her first intimacy with him be less than perfect bliss. He would show her he craved her pleasure far more than he craved his, that his pleasure would always stem from hers.

He tore away from her, snatched his fetters away then stopped. Stood transfixed. Stared at her.

He'd struggled to respect her helplessness when he'd covered her nakedness in the tent. And when he'd tended her in her sickness, his male hormones had been buried under gallons of stress. *Now* he looked.

She'd wrenched an unprecedented response from him when she'd been disguised as a man. He'd thought her the most beautiful creature in creation when he'd seen only her exquisite head and hands. She'd had him balancing on an edge both distressing and intoxicating with glimpses at her assets. But now...

Now he could see himself truly devouring her.

Encased in golden, glowing skin, taut and tight everywhere, her breasts were turgid and peaked, her thighs and hips full and firm, her waist impossible amidst her voluptuousness.

And he could no longer just look, he needed to experience all that, claim it, wallow in it.

"*Rao'ah, jenan...*" He growled, filling his hands with sunlight and gold and honey made woman. *His* woman. "A marvel, madness—beauty like this shouldn't have been sanctioned by the heavens."

"Look who's talking," she moaned as he took the mounds of her breasts into kneading hands, yearning for their weight and feel.

He felt he'd blow an artery without a taste. He bent to have it, laved their peaks, answered their demand for the pull of his suckles, the grazing of his nips.

"*Elahati*, my goddess." He swept her up into his arms, didn't register the journey to the platform bed. He laid her on it, arranged her limbs as if they were flowers, tracing every line demarcating her tawny tan from her still-creamy areas with his tongue. "We'll sunbathe naked from now on. I want to see your inner lioness fully manifested. We'll do anything and everything."

A peach flush evened out her color and her eyes turned almost black as she writhed. "Yes...please, anything... everything..."

The totality of her hunger and trust shot to his heart, tampering with its rhythm. He anchored her as she began to buck beneath him, his fingers lost in the mindless pleasure of spanning her sharp concavity, digging into her taut flesh.

She whimpered a white-hot tremolo that attested to a pleasure she couldn't breathe for its power. "Harres, take me...*daheenah*."

Hearing her say *now* in his mother tongue felt like a giant hammer shattering the last pillar of his control. He would later swear he'd heard the shrieking snap of his mind giving way, the howling implosion of restraint's end.

A rumble rolled inside him like distant thunder as he snapped her turquoise panties down her silken legs. She was golden down to her last secret. Rising on his knees, he barely pushed his drawstring pants down enough to release an arousal that was beyond rock now.

The look of feverish hunger, of shocked intimidation on her face made him want to hold back, take it infinitely slow and gentle. And they made him want to ram into her, ride her, grind his flesh into hers until she wept with the closeness, broke with the pleasure, dissolved in the fusion.

Feeling the world receding in a white noise of incoherence he grabbed her thighs, would have pressed them apart if they hadn't fallen wide-open.

She arched, writhed, tried to drag him to her, inside her.

He pulled back, tried to regain control. She was tampering with his sanity, at the verge of destroying it. He could hurt her. Even if he knew he'd pleasure her, too, he had to hold back.

He opened her folds, forged a path between their molten heat, but denying her the full entry she craved. She came off the bed at the first touch of their most intimate flesh. He laved his hardness in her nectar, rubbing her in escalating rhythm, until she was sobbing. He alternated between shallow nudges and circular strokes, over and over and over, teasing without fully taking.

She rose on her elbows, lips open with distressed gasps, her eyes spewing azure wildness and invitation of anything at all he would do to her.

Then he moved in a tighter rhythm until she fell back

on the bed, legs shaking wide, her back bowed deep as she convulsed into wave after wave of a screeching orgasm.

Seeing her lost to pleasure, pleasure he'd brought her, made his heart thunder with pride, with relief, with uncontrollable lust for more. He was already addicted to the sight, to the experience. He wanted it again. And he set about having it.

He stroked her swollen flesh, soothing it, desensitizing it. Drenched in tears and satiation, yet darkening with a deeper hunger, a wilder need, her eyes seethed as she watched him perform those ultimate intimacies on her, owning her flesh, manipulating her responses, extracting her ecstasy.

Soon, her pleas were a litany. "No, no more…more, you…you…take me, take me, *daheenah,* now, *now…*"

"*Aih*, now. I will take you now, finish you, claim you, brand you. I will plunder you and pleasure you until you weep with the satisfaction, *ya talyeti.*"

He rose onto his knees, kicked off his pants, cupped her buttocks in his hands, tilted her, opened her petals. He started to invade her…and it hit him like a sledgehammer.

He *couldn't* take her.

He almost keeled over her with the realization.

He did slump over her, his head to her breasts, his whole frame shuddering.

She cried out, tried to drag him up, but he resisted her, raised his head, the words cutting him on their way out. "When we get back to the capital. I can only take you fully then." He smoothed the look of distress off her brow, rasped, "But I'll pleasure you now, in so many other ways."

Understanding dawned in the pieces of heaven she had trapped in her eyes. Then a slow, sensuous smile spread her lips. She clamped her legs around his back, pulled him up. He acquiesced, slid over her slippery ripeness, mingling their moans and shudders and sweat.

Once he reached her lips, she gave a throaty moan of scorching seduction. "You *can* take me now. It's safe. For at least a week. You can trust me. I'm a doctor."

So it was a safe time for her. He almost wished it wasn't, and he'd take her knowing that.

If it was up to him, he was sure. He wanted it all with her, now, no waiting. He needed her to know, everything.

"I trust you, *ya habibati,* with my life. And more. And I only cared, for you." She nodded, her eyes adoring him into oblivion, the perfection of her belief pouring fuel on his conflagration. He filled his hands with her, unconditional love made flesh of his flesh. "And I'm safe, too."

She nipped his chin, as if chastising him for needing to voice this. She believed he would never endanger her in any way, didn't need to be told.

And she was opening her arms for him to fill, her beloved body quivering, her every cherished feature emanating her need in bludgeoning waves.

It was too much. He wanted too much. All of her. At once.

His growl sounded frightening in his ears as he sank his teeth anywhere in her flesh on a blind swoop. They dug in where her neck flowed into her soft, strong shoulder like that time during their ordeal when her nearness had meant life. She jerked and threw her head back, giving him a better bite. He took it.

He was a hairbreadth from going berserk. He tried to rein in the frenzy.

Then she made rationing his passion impossible.

"Show me how much you want me." Her voice reverberated in his brain, dark and deep. Wild. "Give me everything, take everything, ride me, finish me. I can't bear the emptiness... *fill* me."

With a growl of surrender he stabbed his fingers into

her short locks, pulled her head back for his devouring. She
bombarded him with a cry of capitulation and command. He
drove her into the thin mattress with a bellow of conquering
lust. And on one staggering thrust, he embedded himself
all the way to her womb.

They arched back. Backs taut, steep curves. Mouths
opened on soundless screams at the potency of the moment.
On pleasure too much to bear. Invasion and captivation.
Completion. At last.

His roar broke through his muteness as he withdrew.
She clutched at him with the tightness of her hot, fluid
femininity, her delirious whimpers and her nails in his
buttocks demanding his return. He met her eyes, saw
everything he needed to live for.

He rammed back against her clinging resistance, his
home inside her. The pleasure detonated again. Her cry
pierced his being. He thrust, hard, harder, until her cries
stifled on tortured squeals. Then she bucked. Ground herself
against him. Convulsed around him in furious, helpless
rhythms, choking out his name, her eyes streaming with
the force of her pleasure.

He rode her to quivering enervation. Then showed her
the extent of his need, her absolute hold over him.

He bellowed her name and his surrender to her as he
found his life's first true and profound release, ecstasy
frightening in magnitude, convulsing in waves of pure
culmination, jetting his seed into her depths until he felt
he'd dissolved inside her.

But even as he sank into her quivering arms, instead of
being satiated, he was harder, hungrier than before.

Which didn't matter. He had to give her time to
recover.

He tried to withdraw. She only wound herself tighter
around him, cried out, clung to him.

"There will be more, and more, soon, and always." He breathed the fire of his erotic promise into her mouth. "Rest now."

She breathed her pleasure inside him, thrust her hips to take him deeper inside her. "I can only if you stay inside me. I can't get enough of you, *ya harresi*."

"Neither will I of you…ever." She was driving him deeper into bondage. He loved it. He drove back into her and she pulsed her sheath around him until he groaned. "Tormentress. But just wait. I, too, will drive you to insanity and beyond."

In response to his erotic menace, she tossed her arms over her head, arched her vision of a body, thrust her tormenting breasts against his chest and purred low with aggressive surrender.

Still jerking with the electrocuting release, he turned her around, brought her over him, her shudders resonating with his.

"Give me your lips, *ya talyeti*…" he gasped, needing the emotional surrender to complete the carnal abandon.

She groped for his lips, fed him her life and passion. Then her lips stilled, still fused to his, as sleep claimed her.

Only then did he let go. And he slept. Truly slept for the first time since he'd gone to rescue her.

She wanted to lie on him forever.

For the past four days she'd gone to sleep like that, after nights of escalating pleasure and abandon.

She propped herself up to wallow in his splendor.

Unbelievable. That just about summed him up.

Just looking at him, her heart tried to burst free of its attachments and her breath wouldn't come until she bent closer to draw it mingled with his beloved scent.

He smiled in his sleep, rumbled, *"Ahebbek."*

I love you. She caught his precious pledge in an open-mouthed kiss. He instantly stirred, dauntingly aroused, returned the kiss then took it over, took her over.

"Ahebbak," she gasped her acute pleasure and total love, as he swept her around, bore her down and thrust into her, knowing he'd find her ready and unable to wait. Their hunger was always too urgent at first, it took only a few greedy tastes of each other, a few unbridled thrusts, to have them convulsing in each other's arms, their pleasure complete.

After the ecstasy he drove her to demolished and re-formed her around him, he twisted again to bring her over him.

He sighed in contentment. *"Aashagek."*

He'd explained what that meant. *Eshg* was a concept that had no equivalent in English. More comprehensive than love, too carnal for adoration and as reverent as worship. It fit perfectly.

"Wana aashagak." She rose over him, took a deep breath. "And I can't believe I thought of this only minutes ago, but I wasn't in any condition to think of anything beyond you." She knew this would intrude on the perfection. But she had to say it. "I want you to know everything."

Harres stiffened beneath her. She frowned in alarm as he disentangled himself from their fusion, sat up. It was one of the few times she'd seen him totally serious.

"This time is ours, *ya nadda jannati*. We will not bring anything or anyone into it. Plenty of time for that when we rejoin the world. Now only you and I matter, *ya malekat galbi*."

Talia shivered at the intensity of passion that permeated his voice. He'd just called her the owner of his heart. By now, she was certain she was.

She was also certain it wouldn't matter.

When they rejoined the world, it would tear them apart.

There was only one thing to do now. Cling as hard as she could to her remaining time with him. And tell him what he needed to know. "I need to tell you."

His golden eyes were explicit with his aversion to letting the world intrude on them now instead of later. But he finally squeezed them shut, giving his reluctant consent.

And she started. "A month ago, I got a letter. It was addressed to Todd. He'd been living with me since he came back from Azmahar, before his conviction. All his mail comes to my house, and I take it to him when I visit. But something made me open this one. Two things. That all mail so far carried only more bad news, and I decided that this time, I'd try to do something about it and tell him only if I failed. The other reason was that it had Zohaydan stamps."

His eyes went dark. He just nodded for her to go on.

"I didn't know what to expect, but it certainly wasn't what I found." She shuddered again with the memory of the explosive emotions the letter had elicited. "The writer said he knew who was involved in framing Todd, that he could expose them, exonerate him. He asked that Todd come to Zohayd, where he'd supply him with the information. He had a huge stake in exposing them, too, but he needed it to be at a stranger's hand. And who better than someone they'd so deeply wronged?

"I realized only after I'd read the letter a dozen times that the writer didn't know Todd was in no position to fulfill his demand. There was an email included, so they could drum out details of the 'mission,' as he called it. I wrote an email explaining the situation, but accepting their mission in Todd's place. Then, right before I hit Send, I reconsidered.

If the writer knew Todd was already convicted, he might give up on the whole thing. And from Todd's reports on the region, I thought he would balk at doing business with a woman. Not to mention that a female foreigner on her own would draw too much attention, all of the unwanted variety. And my plan formed.

"If this person didn't know Todd was in prison, then I could go as him. I had his passport, and I could pass for him with some disguise. I created a new email with Todd's name, emailed him with my acceptance. I got a response within an hour. All I had to do was buy a plane ticket to anywhere in the world to get into the airport's departure gates. Someone would meet me with a pass to a private-jet flight, so I could slip into the region without record of my entry. That worried me, about my departure, but I rationalized they would want me to leave, to carry out their exposé for them. I thought I could also run to the American Embassy if I got into trouble.

"They brought me here. I demanded the info I came for, and my contact told me it was bigger than I thought, that 'my' problems were a part of something that could not only exonerate 'me' but that would destroy the Aal Shalaans, as they deserved to be. Then he called on the cell phone they'd given me. He used one of those electronic voice distorters, said he couldn't afford to ever be linked to what he was about to reveal, wouldn't leave anything to be tracked back to him. And he told me about the stolen and counterfeited Pride of Zohayd jewels, and the consequences that would have for the Aal Shalaans and their regime. I asked how that would help 'me' and he only said I was a bright lad, would work out how to use that info to my benefit. When I started to protest, he said he was in a very sensitive position, had to go now or risk exposure, but that he'd call me later with more info.

"I emailed Mark Gibson, Todd's lawyer and our childhood friend, to ask his opinion. I didn't specify what my contact had told me, just that I possessed info that could bring the royal house of Zohayd down. Two hours later, I was snatched from my rented condo. The next thing I remember was waking up in that hole in the desert. The rest you know."

Then she felt silent. And realized that tears were streaming down her face. Reliving those past events and anticipating even more anguish and hopelessness, not only for Todd but for her and Harres in the future, broke her heart.

Harres's bleak eyes were eloquent with his acknowledgment of the validity of her trepidation. He said nothing, just pulled her back into his arms. Soon, he was kissing her, inflaming her, taking her with a new edge of recklessness, of desperation.

The dread that their time together was counting down to a crushing end made their hunger explosive, their mating almost violent, their ecstasy almost damaging.

Afterward, she lay curved into his body, quivering with the enormity of it all. He pretended to be asleep. She knew he wasn't.

She couldn't sleep, either.

She wondered, once she lost him, if she'd ever sleep again.

As night deepened, the oasis's unique environment somehow warded off the bitter cold of the desert. Even if it had been as bone-chilling as it had been during their trek, Harres wouldn't have felt a thing. He was burning up, from the inside out.

She'd finally fallen asleep. He'd left her side, gone out to try to find air to breathe.

He couldn't find any in the vastness around him.

He stumbled to a stop at the far edge of the cottage's garden, stared up at the preternaturally clear and steady stars. They blurred, swam. The heat seething inside him was filling his eyes with the moisture of frustration and despondence. Just as he'd seen in hers. It had hurt, still did, like a knife in his gut.

What hurt more was that he couldn't wipe those feelings away. He couldn't promise her what he wasn't certain he could deliver. Promises now would torment her with hope. That was even more agonizing than resignation, and if for any reason he failed to keep them, the crash to despair would be far more devastating.

He *would* do whatever it took to secure her happiness. But until he did, he had to keep silent, had to suffer her suffering. And love her with all of his being.

He only prayed it wouldn't come down to a choice between him and her brother.

He couldn't afford to lose her. He wouldn't survive it.

Eleven

Talia lurched awake, the ferocity and satisfaction of Harres's last possession humming in her blood, in her bones.

She stretched, moaning at the delicious frisson of soreness zigzagging through her. He *had* kept his promise of driving her to insanity and beyond. She now thought sanity, like the soul she felt he'd claimed, was a highly overrated and mostly inconsequential trimming.

He wasn't there. But he would be any second.

She rose, freshened up. Just as she finished, she heard the steady clatter of Reeh's hooves at the back of the cottage.

She rushed to the door. The moment she stepped out, gazing up into the twilight of the skies she'd come to depend on seeing, a meteor flashed bright then faded, as if it had never been.

It felt like their time together.

But they didn't behave as if it would ever fade. They both pretended this was forever.

He rode around the cottage, approached her with the smile that was everything worth living for. She rushed to him and he pulled her up on Reeh's back, molded her back to his front, enveloped her within his hot, hard body.

After a while of trotting leisurely in their daily excursion to *al ain,* Talia sighed, snuggled back into the cherishing heat and protection.

"I've come to a conclusion," she announced. He kissed the top of her head, held her more securely, waiting for her revelation. "Getting kidnapped was the best thing that ever happened to me."

He chuckled, hugged her exuberantly. "What a coincidence, since it turned out to be the best thing that ever happened to *me*."

She sighed, knowing he meant it, nuzzled back into his embrace, soaking up his feel, assimilating it into her being along with his scent, mingled with those of the pristine nature.

Then she teased, "Do you think it's possible I'll get to ride my own horse one day?"

"I have issues with seeing you in danger."

"What danger? Horses here, like the rest of the inhabitants, human or otherwise, are wonderfully understanding of inept foreigners."

"Then I have issues about keeping you in my arms for as long as possible…." He stopped, groaned, amended. "Having you in my arms at every opportunity."

She knew he must be kicking himself for phrasing it that way, for even hinting that their time together would come to an end.

She swerved from the subject, turned lips tingling with the numbness of fear into his neck. "A noble cause."

She felt a ragged breath empty his lungs as he gave her a tighter squeeze, as if to thank her for circumventing the emotional landmine. "None higher. I got addicted to holding you like this, ever since I rode back to the oasis with you."

"Buttuli." She tilted her head back to smile up into his eyes and caught the bleakness there.

Tenderness replaced it, making her wonder if she'd even seen it. But she had. And she wouldn't bring it up.

What was the point of worrying about the future but to taint the purity of happiness they shared in the present?

She rubbed the hair he'd told her he adored, called spun gold milled from sunshine, against his bare chest. Now that he no longer wore a bandage but a local dressing over his fast-healing wound, she'd been wallowing in the sensory nirvana of touching his sculptured perfection at every opportunity. Which was almost always.

"Harres…"

"Yes, Talia, say my name like that, like you can't draw another breath if you don't have me inside you. As I will be, here and now."

The blow of arousal at the thought of him carrying out his intention, here, was paralyzing. And not just because it was a fantasy she'd thought would forever go unfulfilled. They were out in the open, with the oasis people in the distance.

She thought he was only stimulating her, that he'd wait until they were by the *ain,* where they'd shared more than one explosive if hurried mating, but then he lifted her, dragged her voluminous dress from beneath her, let it flow over his lap.

Then, as one hand held the bridle, the other slid around to dip below the folds of the neckline, seeking her breasts. Fire forked to her core as his fingers manipulated her nipples. It burst into flames when he sank his teeth in her nape, like a lion securing his mate.

She swooned back, her already open thighs falling apart wider, moisture dampening her panties.

"Do you know what scenting your arousal does to me?" He growled in her ear as his hand slid inside her panties, his palm gently squeezing her for a moment, winding the rhythm of the throbbing there into a frantic pounding. "I want to taste you again, but I'll have to settle for feeling your heat and your satiny flesh as it softens and melts for me. Show me how much you crave my touch, *ya talyeti*."

Beyond caring that they might be seen, she bucked back against him, widening her thighs, giving him full access. "I'm out of my mind craving anything you do to me, all the time. Touch me, feel for yourself, do everything to me."

With a groan of male possession, he dipped a finger along the molten lips of her sex, sliding its thickness and power on a mind-numbing path to and fro, each pass tightening the coil of agonizing pleasure inside her. She writhed, whimpered, turned her face up to his. He thrust his tongue inside her mouth as he replaced his finger with his thumb and plunged his middle finger inside her. The coil snapped, and she unraveled around him, in his arms on bucking keens. He stroked her inner trigger, stoked it until the climax drained her of the frenzy he'd built inside her.

"Having you lost to pleasure is the most magnificent thing I've ever experienced," he rumbled against her mouth as his fingers still stroked her, avoiding her sensitive bud, until he soothed her, then he changed direction and rhythm, had her climbing to mindlessness again.

Once she was begging, she felt him release himself, his hard length slamming against her buttocks. He whispered in her ear, "Rise up with your thigh muscles like I taught you in the trot."

He was really going to take her here. Like this. The idea almost drove her over another edge.

She rose up and he positioned himself at her opening.

He was saying, "Settle down on me," when her muscles jellified. She crashed down on him.

He forged through her inner folds like a hot lance. She thought she'd gotten used to his length and girth, but it seemed that every time felt like the first time, felt as if he filled her more.

Now the pressure reached an edge of pain, of domination that redefined all her concepts of physical intimacy and pleasure. She was addicted to the impossible fullness, the feeling of total occupation, of trapping such a vital part of him so inescapably inside her and drawing both their pleasure from depths she—and he insisted he, too—hadn't known existed.

By the fourth or fifth buck and fall of the trot she was a mass of tremors, fully at his power, breached to her core, invaded, occupied, pleasured, taken, maddened.

"Ride me…ride me…" was all she could say anymore, all that was left in her mind. She was enervated with an overload of sensation, the pressure becoming beyond her endurance. She needed him to thrust her to release. Before anyone passed.

He only lay back into the trot, let its rhythm layer even more sensation. All the time, he said things that drove her deeper into bondage. "Filling you this way, invading you, being captured by you is all I can think of, I want to be home, inside you, pleasuring you, always…."

And she found another word. *"Please."*

She felt him jerk inside her, grow bigger. She keened, writhed, and he growled, nudged Reeh, pounded into her with all the fury of the gallop. Just when she thought her heart would stop and she would dissolve around him and be no more, his fingers massaged her bud in escalating circles, his teeth sinking into her neck again, his growls a carnal current knotting her heart and core. And she detonated.

A scream welled from her depths, too frenzied to form. The next one would have but he caught it in his palm, gave her his flesh to vent her agonized pleasure on.

She bit into the side of his palm, over and over as breaker after breaker of release crashed through her, receded, built only to smash into her again, scattering and reforming her for the next incursion. The convulsions radiated from the deepest point within her body, which he caressed, spread in expanding shock waves, each building where the last began to diminish. Then he plumbed a new depth in her, seeming to impale her to her heart, releasing his ecstasy there. Feeling him fill her to overflowing sent her thrashing once more. She wished…she wished…

She regained lucidity with a jerk. They'd reached *al ain*. He was still inside her. The pleasure was a continuous flow now, a plateau of contentment. Her head rolled limply over his heart.

"You should have told me you won't just drive me insane, you'll regularly knock me out, too."

He chuckled, a sound of profound male smugness. "I live to please."

She shuddered as he separated their fusion. "And how."

He adjusted his clothes and jumped off the horse, holding out his arms for her. "And no one saw us."

She closed her eyes in mortification. She couldn't believe she'd risked that. He did drive her insane.

His smile became pure bedevilment. "Let's hope for better luck next time."

* * *

There was no next time.

It was almost sunset the next day when she felt a bass drone reverberate in her bones.

In moments the distant yet approaching thunder became unmistakable. A helicopter.

Harres's people had come for them.

Their idyll had come to an end.

Harres turned to her, his eyes eloquent with the same sentiments. But he attempted a smile. "They'll be here in minutes. Do you want to leave immediately?"

She didn't want to leave at all.

She only said, "Yes."

He nodded. "Let's gather the stuff the oasis people gave us."

"I only wish I had something to give them, too."

"You gave them far more than souvenirs, made a lasting difference in so many lives. Many told me they were blessed the day the desert 'yielded you to them.' And you can bring them whatever you want later." She gasped. Then he articulated her wildest hope. "We'll be back here, *ya nadda jannati*. I promise."

In fifteen minutes, she was standing with Harres a hundred feet from the clearing where the helicopter had just landed.

Four men jumped down, walked toward them with movements made of power and purpose, not even acknowledging the brutal wind buffeting them from the still-storming rotors.

As they strode closer, Talia was left in no doubt they were Harres's blood.

Apparently Aal Shalaan men all descended from a

line that had originated the oriental fables of supernatural beings.

The men were close enough to be classed in the same level, yet different enough as to be totally distinct from one another.

But it was the man who'd been in the pilot's seat who captured and kept her focus. And not because she recognized him as Zohayd's crown prince.

Amjad Aal Shalaan had an aura about him that lashed out across space and punched air from an onlooker's body. He reminded her of a majestic black panther, perpetually coiled for attack, complete with startling, searing, soulless emerald eyes. And he had those eyes trained on hers. She could swear she felt her eyeballs about to combust before he turned his attention to his brother.

But that brief eye-lock had been enough for her to have no doubt. He was nothing like Harres. That perfect body housed a dangerous, merciless entity. No one got a second chance with Crown Prince Amjad Aal Shalaan. She doubted anyone got a first one.

For the next few minutes she watched as those male manifestations of the forces of nature descended on Harres with relief and affection. All but Amjad. He held back, his gaze on her.

She felt him slicing through the layers of her character like a mental CAT scan, cutting to her essence like a psychic laser.

Harres introduced the others, Munsoor, Yazeed and Mohab—the latter Ghada's reluctant fiancé—as the cousins who'd been with him for her retrieval operation. They shook hands with her, expressed their pleasure to see her well, if not exactly who they'd signed on to save. They exchanged with Harres dozens of questions and reports about what had happened since they got separated twenty days ago.

Suddenly Amjad spoke. "Enough with the reunion. You can all debrief each other, or whatever you do in this secret-service game you play, later." He focused on Harres. "After Shaheen spent the last three weeks tearing the kingdom apart with me looking for you, he couldn't waste one more moment away from his bride coming to fetch you and has jumped back into her embrace. He sends his 'love' from its depths."

Harres's lips twisted at him. "You tore apart the kingdom looking for me? I'm so touched. I hope we can now glue it back together."

Amjad shot him a look of demolishing sarcasm. She was sure a lesser man than Harres would have shriveled up. "The trials and tribulations of the oldest brother and all that. And then I couldn't let you get lost in the desert with my vital info, now could I? You can glue things back together yourself. Cleanup detail is why a man puts up with younger siblings."

Talia's mouth fell open. Harres only hugged her to his side and guffawed. "*Aih,* I love you, too, Amjad."

Amjad's gaze clamped the unit she and Harres formed.

Then he grimaced, rolled his eyes before leveling them on Harres disgustedly. "Not you, too."

Harres only laughed. "Oh, definitely me, too. And I hereby echo Shaheen's words. I can't wait until you make it three."

Amjad dismissed him like one would an insignificant annoyance, turned to her. Then, as he looked directly into her eyes, he talked about her in third person. "So what does she have over the rest of the women in the northern hemisphere? Since you went through them all, I'd be very interested to know what extra features she has installed that made you shed your sanity."

Harres nudged Amjad's shoulder, pointing to his own eyes with two fingers. "Eyes here, Amjad."

Amjad ignored him, kept looking at her, yet talking about her, not to her. "The way she's glaring back at me. Fascinating. Fearless, is she? Or is she just so perceptive that she read you right, knew she could pretend fearlessness knowing she has nothing to fear, and that would be what gets to you?"

This time Harres sort of punched him. "Quit your snide mother-in-law routine, Amjad, or prepare to eat some sand."

Amjad's sculpted lips twisted, the provocation in his gaze only rising as he looked down at her. "First you let Shaheen sink into Johara's thrall without throwing so much as a cursory rope and now you're eagerly rushing to join the collective of beached men. Is she pregnant, too? At least, was she any good..." Amjad allowed a beat for her to start to seethe, for Harres to take offense for real before he continued smoothly. "...for any info we can use?"

Okay. All right. The verdict was in.

They hired this guy to teach goading in hell.

The other three men had slipped away midconfrontation, went back to the helicopter to prepare it for the return flight. And, no doubt, to give the brothers a chance to have at it.

Though Amjad was formidable, Harres was clearly the more physical one and there was no doubt who would win in a fight. That was, if Amjad didn't fight dirty. Which she was sure he would, and did.

Keeping her hand clasped in his, Harres said with Amjad's same lethal tranquility, "I'll say this once, Amjad. Talia is my woman, my princess." Talia almost collapsed. Harres was saying what he wished for, wasn't taking into account the implausibility of it all. It felt like heaven. And like hell. And he was going on. "I owe her my life, and I

have no life without her from now on. Deal with it. Nicely.
Or else."

Suddenly Amjad addressed her. "See this? Your man,
your prince, hits a snag, and he threatens, and may I add,
employs, physical violence. Tut, tut. A bleak prognosis for a
future with him, don't you think, doctor?" Then he swung
his eyes to Harres. "And I had such high hopes for you.
Have fun in your new life of mind-numbing sameness and
soul-destroying emotional servitude."

Before she could finally set him straight, on so many
accounts, before Harres could elaborate on his gag order,
Amjad turned away, gave the oasis people who'd come to
say goodbye a whimsical wave and headed back to the
helicopter.

Then, as Talia hugged everyone who came to see her
off, crying rivers with Harres beside her promising their
return, the aggravating man had the nerve to honk.

Talia's return to the capital was the total reverse of her
departure from it.

Going back in a royal helicopter surrounded by princes
was certainly something she couldn't have even dreamed of
when she'd been kidnapped twenty days ago. But being next
to Harres as the real world approached made her realize
the depth and breadth of the lifetime they'd lived together
during that time.

After they landed in the princes' private airport, Talia
changed into the clothes Harres had had delivered there,
while he changed, too, before they drove to the palace in
separate limos.

He told her they couldn't afford to have her tied to him.
Apart from those who knew the truth, everyone thought he'd
dropped off the radar on a mission as usual. But the traitors
in the palace would know what this mission involved. If she

were seen with him, they'd work out her true identity. So she'd arrive at the palace as a friend of Laylah, his cousin. Once that was established, he'd pretend to hook up with her, and it would seem natural to everyone that he'd be interested in the blonde beauty.

She told him she'd reconnect with her informant, get the rest of the promised info. And he forbade her to. He wouldn't risk her in any way, not even if the kingdom hung in the balance. He would find another way to discover the truth.

Then, reluctant to leave her but having matters to attend to, he gave her a cell phone so they could call each other until he could start seeing her again. Which he intended to be as soon as possible.

It took arriving at the palace—which was right up there with the Taj Mahal, just far more extensive—to take her mind off the turmoil of their situation, off feeling bereft at being away from him.

When she'd researched Zohayd before coming there, she'd read that the mid-seventeenth-century palace had taken more than three decades to build, and thousands of artisans and craftsmen to build it. But it was one thing looking at detailed photos, no matter how stunning they'd been, and something totally different treading this place with her own feet, feeling the history and grandeur saturating the walls and halls surround her, permeating her senses.

Just being there explained so much about Harres, how such a powerhouse had come into existence. The nobility and power and distinction, the ancient bloodline that had forged this place coursed through him. From what she'd seen of his relatives, it also did in them.

And no matter what he said, she had to do all she could to protect this legacy. Even if she hadn't fallen in love with him and would therefore do anything to protect him and his loved ones, Harres had been right. The whole kingdom was steeped in peace and prosperity. She'd been prejudiced when she'd thought that it would be better off without the royal family that had clearly done so much to produce and maintain that.

But if she played her cards right, she might help bring the danger to Harres and his family, to the kingdom and the whole region, to an end.

Just as she began to call her informant, reinitiating contact, her alibi for her long absence rehearsed, the phone came alive in her hand.

Knowing it was Harres, she pounced on the answer button.

His beloved voice poured into her ear. "I have news, *ya habibati*. The investigations and negotiations I had my family do while we were in the oasis bore fruit. Your brother will be released from prison. There won't be a retrial, just the charges dropped and he will be given a public apology in every international newspaper and anything he demands in compensation."

To say she was overcome would be to say her love for him was a passing fancy. She began to babble her shocked elation and thanks when he said, "I beg your forgiveness, *ya nadda jannati*. There is another pressing thing I have to attend. I'll call again the second I can. Until then, congratulations, *ya mashoogati*."

She stared at the phone, reeled. Todd. Released. It was over. Really over. She'd have her brother back. He'd have his life back. It was too much to take in. Harres hadn't told her that he'd been working to exonerate Todd already. But he had been, and he'd succeeded. And she knew it had all been for her.

She fell on the bed and curled into a tight ball. She

felt she might explode from too much love and relief and gratitude otherwise.

Then she burst up in a frenzy of purpose, dialed the number of her informant. She was told the number was no longer in service. She tried again, just to make sure she hadn't dialed it wrong. She hadn't. It must have been a temporary number so it couldn't be tracked. On the same thought, she went online, shot him an email, listing her phone number.

Moments after she hit Send, the phone's distinctive three-tone ring shot through her again. Harres. He must have more info.

Her flailing hand dropped it twice before she could answer. Then she almost dropped it again.

It wasn't Harres. It was a distorted voice that scraped her every nerve raw. Her informant's.

She hadn't dreamed he'd get back to her that fast. But it wasn't that that shocked her mute. It was what he'd said.

"Hello, Dr. Talia Jasmine Burke."

She squeezed her eyes. So their precautions hadn't worked. She didn't know how, but her cover was blown.

"Don't worry, doctor. I still want to do business with you. You're now in an even better situation to do the most damage. Harres is doing all he can to stay on your good side, to exploit you, so I hope you aren't falling for his charm and forgetting your original goal to redeem your brother." At her gasp, the distorted voice gave a macabre chuckle. "Yes, I know everything. That's why I went after you in the first place. Because I wanted someone with a cause, and because you are a woman. It suits me to have the Aal Shalaan's downfall be at the hands of someone who has a vendetta against them, and who better than a woman to bring all those mighty men to ruin.

"And now, I'll tell you who the mastermind behind the

conspiracy is. Yusuf Aal Waaked, prince of the neighboring emirate of Ossaylan."

Talia at last found her voice. "But why expose him and risk having the Aal Shalaans stop the conspiracy in its tracks once they learn who they have to fight and where they need to look for their missing jewels?"

"Oh, there's nothing the Aal Shalaans can do with his identity. My exposure will actually guard against him changing his mind. It will guarantee he'll see this through to the end."

Suddenly there was a long silence then the voice became uglier, scarier. "You idiot! You'll use the info to help Harres, won't you? He *has* gotten to you. I should have known, with a woman in the legendary playboy prince's clutches for so long. He must have you willing to sell your soul for him by now. But I'll prove to you that he and his family don't deserve your help, but your vengeance."

The line went dead.

She didn't know how long she'd stayed there, staring into space, shaking with agitation.

At last she roused herself. She had to call Harres, give him the new info. No matter what her informant said, she was sure Harres *would* do something with it, maybe solve this whole mess.

As she began to dial his number, two masked men burst into the room from the French doors that opened to a patio leading to the gardens. The gun in the first's hand made sure she didn't attempt a scream or a struggle.

"We won't harm you," the armed man said, "if you don't try to expose us. We just want you to come with us. There's something our master wants to show you."

They took her from the French doors, swept her around the palace through the extensive grounds.

They entered through another open French door into

a room. It was empty. Before she could say anything, she heard Harres's voice.

Her heart fired with hope, then dread crashed right on its heels. What if he walked in here, and they panicked, shot him?

But then she realized he wasn't moving. He was in an adjoining room, talking to someone. On the phone.

"...and how many women have you seen me take and discard? You think this American means more than any of them? The others at least were pleasant pastimes I remember with some goodwill. She, on the other hand, almost cost me my life. Can you even imagine the distaste I suffered as I catered to her for so long, struggled to save her miserable life, to get her to trust me and spill her secrets, and to change her mind about exposing them? Do you realize how enraged I was when I found out she knew practically nothing? But I had to continue to play along. I knew she could still renew her mission and secure the rest of the promised info."

He was silent for a moment, then he drawled, his voice pitiless, "Why do you think I gave her the trivial incentive of setting her brother free? She trusts me with her life now, will do anything to get me my coveted intel. I went so far as to proclaim my love, would have even offered to marry her if necessary."

He was silent for a moment more as the person on the other line interrupted him. Then Harres gave an ugly laugh, a sound she'd never thought could issue from him. "I might have afforded a measure of chivalry and human compassion in other circumstances. But anyone is expendable in my quest to fulfill my duty to protect this kingdom. So if she's useless to me on that front, do you really think I care if she lives or dies?"

Twelve

"Did you hear enough, *ya ghabeyah?*"

Ghabeyah. Stupid.

She'd been far beyond that.

She was beyond devastated.

The nightmarish voice continued. "That's what your prince says when he's having a private conversation with his crown prince, who's taking him to task over you. That's the ugly truth of his feelings. Still want to run to him with the information? Or will you now finally take the revenge you're owed?"

Talia stared at the phone on the bed. Who'd turned it on? How had she made it back to this room?

Her eyes panned around, unseeing. She was alone.

Her escorts must have led her back, turned on the phone's speaker. Their master, her informant, was pulling at the hook embedded inside her, shredding her insides.

Then at some point, the mutilation stopped. And silence decimated what was left intact of her.

She found herself on her side on the bed, a discarded body paralyzed with pain too huge to register yet. Her eyes were open and bone-dry. Harres's words revolved like a serrated wheel inside her skull, mashing her brain to tinier fragments.

He didn't mean it. Whimpers of denial spun in a countering direction. *There's an explanation. He was placating Amjad, his odious brother, to get him off his back, off my case. Or something. It must have killed him to say those things. He'll explain why he did. He loves me. I won't believe otherwise...*

"Talia."

Harres. Here? Or in her feverish hopes?

She jerked up. He *was* here. Looking down at her.

Please, my love, take it back, explain it away. Just look at me with love in your eyes and it will all go away.

But for the first time since she'd laid eyes on him, his were empty.

No. Give me something.

He gave her nothing, his face as expressionless as his voice. "Sorry to interrupt your rest, but my private jet is ready."

"Ready for what?" She heard her bleeding whisper, wondered how she could still talk.

"To take you home."

She stared up at him, the void emanating from him engulfing her. Then she found herself rising, as if a closer look would make her see inside him, decipher the truth.

She saw nothing. Only the abyss of uncaring he'd professed to feel for her.

And it all crashed down on her, the full weight of his betrayal, of his heartless exploitation. It crushed her.

But she realized one thing. Even hurt beyond expression or endurance, injured beyond healing, she couldn't retaliate in kind. She wouldn't. This was the one thing her informant hadn't taken into consideration in his quest to destroy the Aal Shalaans.

Harres had systematically destroyed her, for his duty, his family. But even had she wanted to exact revenge on him, she wouldn't destroy the royal family and the whole kingdom along with him. And she *didn't* want to avenge herself. She just wanted to curl up and die, far away from this land where she'd lost her heart and her faith in anything forever.

One thing was left in her wreckage. "What about Todd?"

"The procedures of his release are ongoing as we speak."

She saw the truth of this at least in his eyes. Or maybe she imagined it as she'd imagined everything between them so far.

And she gave him what he'd ruined her for. "The conspiracy's mastermind is Yusuf Aal Waaked, prince of Ossaylan."

His eyes flared. But she'd lost the ability to read them. She'd never had it. And she no longer cared. She just wanted out of his orbit. Wanted to go somewhere far to perish in peace.

"I know," he finally said in the same expressionless voice.

He did? How?

One thing explained everything. He'd monitored her phone call and got his coveted information the moment she had.

So the master secret-service man had adjusted his plan on the fly every second since they'd met, according to her reactions and based on an unerring reading of her character. She'd fallen in step with his every undetectable nudge. His masterstroke had been that last bit of reverse psychology. While indirectly stressing the danger Zohayd was in, he'd forbidden her to reinstate contact with her informant, knowing the first thing she'd do was just that. As the coup de grâce, he'd secured Todd's release. It clearly had required no effort or sacrifice on his part, had been insurance to make sure she would do anything for him.

Now her purpose to him was over. He couldn't wait to get rid of her.

It made sense. Far more sense than this all-powerful prince falling in love with her, so totally.

With this last shard of rationalization tearing into her heart, it was like a dampener dissolved and every memory of the past twenty days bombarded her, rewritten in the macabre new perspective.

Agony mushroomed to unmanageable levels, humiliation inundating her. She felt she'd suffocate, shatter.

She lashed out with all her disillusion and devastation. "So you know. But you can't say I didn't give you something in return for my brother's freedom and redemption. Now that I have them, I can't wait to leave this godforsaken land."

There was no mistaking what slammed into his eyes now. Shock.

Of course. He must have thought she'd simper and fawn and beg for him to keep her on any degrading terms he wished to impose. As he'd reassured his brother, he was an old hand at using and discarding women. He must have fully expected the dumping to be one-sided.

Before he could say anything, Amjad stuck his head around the door. "What's taking you so long?"

Harres tore his stunned eyes from hers, turned them to his brother. He still said nothing.

Then he shook his head, as if trying to credit what she'd said. She could only imagine how she'd sounded, looked as she'd said it. If a fraction of what was stampeding inside her had been apparent, he must be flabbergasted at the seemingly out-of-the-blue change that had seized her.

He stood aside, staring at her with eyes crowded with so many things it made her sick trying to fathom them. She gave up, on everything, preceded him out of the room.

Amjad was leaning on the wall outside the door in an immaculate sports jacket, his arms folded over his chest.

As she passed him, his eyes gleamed ruthlessly. "Give my…regards to your brother. He's to be congratulated for having a sister like you."

She stared at him, felt the urge to ask for an explanation. It fizzled out as it formed.

Feeling ice spreading from her center outward, she turned away, let Harres steer her outside the palace.

He sat beside her in his limo, the eerie silence that had replaced their animated conversations, his feigned interest and indulgence, deepening her freeze.

They arrived at the private airport they'd landed in only hours ago. What a difference that time had made.

He rushed out of the limo before it came to a full stop. He materialized on her side in seconds, handed her out of the limo, led her to the sleek silver Boeing 737 purring like a giant alien bird on the pristine tarmac.

His movements were measured, his hold the epitome of composure. The vibes emanating from him were the opposite.

At the stairs he turned to her. But though the move was controlled, his eyes were anything but, storming with emotions barely held in check. His voice sounded even more agitated. "What was that back at the palace?"

It couldn't be just his displeasure at her rewriting his expected dumping scene, could it?

Stop it. She *must* stop casting anything she felt from him through the prism of nobility and sincerity. She'd heard the truth with her own ears. What was she waiting for? To have it said to her face?

She wouldn't survive that. *End this.* Now.

She shrugged, started to turn away, to run away.

His hand snagged hers. But it was the confusion and hurt she thought she saw eclipsing the twin suns of his eyes that stopped her, captured her. "You're saying it was all for your brother? To manipulate me into setting him free?"

How could he still sound so genuine? How could she still be so pathetic that she wanted to believe him, melt into his arms, to answer her walking orders with proclamations of undying love?

Ghabeyah. Stupid. That was what her informant had called her.

No. She wouldn't give him the satisfaction of seeing her weep for him. She was so far beneath him, so disadvantaged, in every way, but especially in the depth of her involvement. She could only try to leave him on equal ground in at least that.

She heard the acid that now filled her arteries drip from her voice. "That wasn't too far to go to make you help an innocent man prove his innocence, don't you think?"

She'd seen him get shot. He hadn't reacted this spectacularly then. After his recoil, he stilled, seeming to loom larger, his vibe darkening until it was deeper than the night enveloping them.

Then he finally snarled, "It is *I* who has gone *far* farther to help a guilty man get away with his crimes."

For a moment she didn't get his meaning. Just as it dawned on her, he gritted out, "I guess committing fraud runs in your family, after all."

She staggered out of his hold. "I didn't think even you would go that far."

"*Even* me? What is that supposed to mean?"

"Nothing. None of it meant anything." She'd crumble at his feet any moment now. *Get away from him.*

She groped for the rails. He caught her back, twisted her around to face him. His face was a conflagration of every distraught emotion humanly achievable.

You're seeing what you want to see.

Pain skewered her, tearing the last tatters of her sanity.

"What is it?" she rasped. "Is your ego smarting? You want me to go but still want me to beg to stay? Or maybe you want another payment for Todd's freedom? On board your jet? I can give you one last go if you want to cross another fantasy off your list, with a reluctant woman this time."

For an eternity, it seemed, horror froze his features. Then his phone rang. He lurched, looked down as if not understanding where the sound was coming from, or its significance.

She broke away from his now loose hold, ran up the stairs. She wanted to keep running, out of her very skin.

Then she had to stop, heaped on the farthest seat in the jet. She begged the first person who came offering her services to please, leave her alone. She wanted nothing.

She only wanted to let the pain eat her up.

And for the duration of the flight toward a home she'd forgotten, a home no longer for now she'd remain forever homeless, she let it.

"Talia! You did it!"

Talia slumped against the door she'd just closed.

Todd.

She swung around, and there he was zooming toward her, his eyes filled with tears as he pounced on her and snatched her into a crushing embrace.

She shook, her battered mind unable to grasp the reality of his presence, here, so soon. How…?

She must have voiced her shock. He pulled back, held her at arm's length, his eyes, so much like hers, unsteady and avid over her face. "How did you do it? Mark told me you were trying to get me out, but I didn't dare hope that you would actually do it."

She almost told him, *I sold my soul to the devil for your freedom.* But that wouldn't be accurate. She'd given her soul of her own free will to said devil. And she'd asked for nothing in return. Todd's freedom hadn't been the price of her soul, just another strand in a convoluted, undetectable web of manipulation.

Yet to see him, free, here, was worth anything.

Not that she could bear more turmoil now, or contact, with even the brother who'd always felt like a physical part of her. Every nerve in her body felt exposed.

She pushed away, shrugged. "It doesn't matter what I did. What's important is that you're free and exonerated."

"How can you say that? I need to know if you got yourself in trouble for me."

"What's important is you're out and can resume your life."

"Oh, God, you did do something terrible, didn't you?" He caught her by the shoulders, his agitation mounting, shaking his whole slight frame. "Whatever you did, undo it. I'll go back to prison, serve the rest of my sentence."

"Don't worry, Todd. I'll deal."

But the lie must have been blatant on her face. Todd's

tears flowed down his shuddering, flushed face. "Please, Talia, take it back. I'm not worth it."

"Of course you are. You're my brother, my twin. And the most important thing is that you're innocent."

"But I'm *not*."

She'd thought she'd depleted her reserves for shock, that all that was left in her was oceans of grief and agony.

She stared at Todd, denial still fighting to ward off comprehension. His next words ended its struggle.

"I—I committed all the crimes I was convicted for. I hacked into accounts I found out about when Ghada once let me fix her computer. She was just a good friend, and I made up the whole thing about us to give you a story you'd believe and sympathize with. I embezzled millions, sold dozens of vital secrets. I did far more than what they found out. But I couldn't admit it to you. It was part shame, part needing you to stand by me, to help me get out of this nightmare. I feared that if you knew I deserved what I got and worse, even with loving me, your sense of honor would stop you from trying. But I no longer care. I'll go back so you can stop paying the price for the freedom I don't deserve. I only hope you can one day forgive me."

She stared at him. This was too much.

It was all a lie.

The two men she loved more than life had both used her and exploited her unconditional love for them.

She tore herself away from Todd's pleading hands.

He sobbed as she staggered away. Before she stumbled into her room, to hide from the world and never exit again, she turned numbly. "Just don't get yourself in trouble again. I don't have any more in me to pay. And what I paid is forever gone."

The heart, the soul, the faith, the will to live.

All gone.

* * *

Seemed she was more resilient than she thought.

At the crack of dawn she was up, crackling with an unstoppable need. To confront Harres.

She'd thought she'd die rather than do it. But when she'd slept, her dreams had crowded with faithful replays of their time together. The contradiction between what she'd lived firsthand and the words she'd heard him say was so staggering, she knew something didn't add up. She hadn't been in any condition to realize that yesterday, too worn-out in every way, too shocked, too ready for bad news, too insecure, too you-name-it, that her mind hadn't functioned properly.

Now she was back to her scientific, logical, gotta-have-answers-that-fit self. More or less. And she would settle this, would ask the question she'd been too raw to ask before.

Why had he said those things?

She'd take any chance that he'd have a perfect explanation and remain the man she loved with all her soul, the memory of whom would enrich her life even if she could never see him again. Far better than believing he had no reason but the obvious one, and was the monster she couldn't bear living believing he was.

So she called him. For six hours straight. His phone was turned off.

Going crazy with frustration, she went back to work. Might as well do something with all this energy that others would benefit from.

She headed to the doctors' room, running on auto. But as she approached, she felt…something.

She shook her head. *Stop daydreaming, T.J.* What would that "something" be doing here?

She squared her shoulders, readying herself for the

storm of interrogation over her sudden month-long leave of
absence when she'd never missed a day of work.

The…premonition expanded with every step. The pull
became irresistible. She knew she'd feel like the stupidest
person in the galaxy in seconds when it turned out to be
all in her mind, but she didn't care. She ran.

She burst into the room.

And there he was.

Harres.

She hadn't been imagining it. She had *felt* him.

Which meant she had an infallible sense where he was
concerned.

Which meant she might have the man she loved back
after all.

He'd been leaning against the table that acted as
the doctors' meeting/dining/sleeping surface, pushing his
tailored jacket out of the way to dip his hands deep into
the pockets of molded-on-him pants, his feet crossed in
deceptive relaxation at the ankles.

He'd always looked incredible. But here, among mundane
surroundings and everyday people, he looked unequivocally
godly. The potency of the ancient pride and the birthright
of power emanating from him swept over her.

He waited until she entered and got a load of him dom-
inating the place, being gaped at by all present, before he
pushed to his feet, oh, so slowly, his eyes lashing out solar
flares.

She imagined herself breaking into a sprint, charging
him, pushing him flat on that table and losing her mind all
over him. A mind that flooded with images and sensations,
of tearing his clothes off as his magical hands rid her of
hers, before raising her as she straddled him, then lowering
her on his…

She swayed with the power of the fantasy. She felt as if

he was transmitting it directly into her brain, generating it, sharing it.

But it was his eyes that snared her in a chokehold. A tiger's. Crackling with scorching…rage? Pain? Both?

One thing was unmistakable. Searing challenge.

He straightened fully, cocked his head at her. "You called?"

"Saw my missed calls, huh?" She turned to her colleagues, who were watching her and Harres like they would their favorite soap. She wouldn't be surprised if someone ran out for popcorn. She twisted her lips at their audacious interest, poked sarcasm at all present, starting with herself. "I accumulated over two hundred. Must be why Prince Harres found a transatlantic visit to be the only suitable way to see what the hell was so pressing."

Taking her cue, showing her that he was embarrassment-proof, he walked up to her with seeming indolence. When he was within arm's length, he lashed out like a cobra, caught her to him, his gaze snaring hers in a fiercer grip.

"So, Dr. T. J. Burke…are you congratulating yourself how I, who could always smell the slightest trace of fraud, ate up your lies and am still back for more?"

She stood in his grip, her heart quivering with unfurling hope. "I never lied. In fact, like you once said, I can't lie. Just ask those guys." Grunts of corroboration issued from everyone around who'd been singed by her inability to hide the truth of her feelings. Suddenly, the pain she'd experienced yesterday welled up inside her. And she pinched him, in the sensitive underside of both arms. Hard. "But *you* lie like a bird can fly."

His frown cracked on a twitch of surprise at her unexpected action, at its sting, on a jerk of humor at her rhyme, before resuming full force. "I never, *ever* lied to you. And if you never did to me, as I would have staked my life on till yesterday, why did you say what you said? Or did you really think you needed to seduce me to get me to help Todd? If you did, didn't you know I would have helped the very devil to make you happy? That you didn't need to say you felt anything for me, because it's enough for me that *I* feel everything for you?"

His words washed over her in healing waves, wiping away all the pain and doubt in swell after swell.

Then she remembered Todd's staggering confession, and her heart compressed. Harres had probably done a host of illegal things to get him off the hook. All for her.

She soothed the flesh she'd abused, her heart brimming with sorrow and remorse. "I was just lashing out in shock and misery."

"Why?" He had the look of a man who was watching his sanity ebbing before his eyes.

She pinched him again, harder this time, dragging a growl from his depths, a mixture of pain and aggravation and arousal. "Because I *heard* you. Saying you don't care if I live or die. So you *were* lying, to someone. That's why I called you. To ask you who you were lying to, and why." She pushed out of his arms, stuck her fists in her waist. "So?"

Harres felt the mountain that had been crushing him since yesterday lifting. This explained everything.

She'd heard him.

"*Ya Ullah.* It's a wonder you didn't kill me and ask questions later." He laughed, with all the discharge of his confusion and agony. "So, the reason I said those things—which, by the way, made me so sick that I haven't been able to put a thing in my mouth since—is I got a phone call, someone telling me they know who you are, what you mean to me, and if I don't back off, they'll harm you. I had to say you meant nothing to me, to make you invalid as a target.

"After I said what I did to my extortionist, I had to keep playing it cool with you since I knew we had traitors in the palace, and your room was probably bugged. I would have explained things to you the moment we were outside monitoring range, but you hit me with that delightful surprise about never feeling anything for me. I couldn't believe it, but you seemed so distant, so different, until I began to lose my mind thinking it might be true. I wouldn't have let you go if Amjad hadn't called at that moment. As it was I sent a dozen men as your security detail just in case."

"So that explains all those *GQ* specimens suddenly hanging around outside my house. Way to go picking guys only I in my condition couldn't see for the elite secret-service agents they are." A smile, sheepish and adoring, trembled on her lips, still echoing pain. He wanted to devour them, soothe away the remainder of her agitation. She bit them, making him feel her teeth had sunk into his own flesh. "I can't tell you how sorry I am for...Todd. I should have suspected something, but I guess I am too stupid when it comes to him."

"I'm not sorry. In fact, I owe your misbehaving brother a debt I can never repay. Your misplaced belief in his innocence drove you to Zohayd and into my life. Amjad and Shaheen pulled some major strings, but I personally paid back with interest everyone he defrauded, and it feels like such a tiny price for having you."

Then she was in his arms, burrowing deep into his chest and deeper into his being and bawling her eyes out.

He filled his aching arms with his every reason for life, every source of happiness. When he'd thought he'd lost her, had never had her... He shuddered. He couldn't even think of those soul-gnawing hours. And he had to tell her something else.

"I'm not here because you called, *ya talyeti*. I was on my way here. That's why you amassed those missed calls. But I am ecstatic that you didn't give up on me, even after hearing the horrors I was forced to utter about you, that you still called, still gave me the benefit of the doubt."

She looked up from the depths of his embrace, her heavenly eyes brimming with love. "How could I not, when I sobered up and remembered what we shared?" She told him about her own phone call, and they both realized at the same moment. She articulated the realization. "My informant masterminded everything. Threatening my safety to you, forcing you to say what you did and forcing me to hear it."

"But that's where he went wrong." He gathered her to him more securely, feeling his heart stagger with the blessing of having her belief, so deep it had withstood that brutal test. And he had no doubt, would stand a lifetime of tests, come what may. As would his. "He didn't count on you being too ethical to lash out by doing his dirty work for him, and loving me so much that you'd give me a chance to exonerate myself."

The adoration in her eyes enveloped him, made him feel invincible. "And he didn't count on you being unable to believe I could use you that way, that you'd come after me, and that we'd talk, get past the doubts and hurt and find each other again."

He suddenly swung her in the air around and around. Her unfettered laughter echoed his overwhelming relief and elation, fell all over him like pearls tinkling off crystal.

He finally put her down, cupped her beloved face in his hands. "And now we have. And with your brother free and no doubt planning to atone, and with us being on the final leg of aborting the conspiracy now that all the pieces are in place, and now that I'm certain the threat against you was just a ploy to get you to hear me and lash out, all our obstacles have been removed." He kneeled in front of her. "I have nothing to give you while I make this offer but everything I am. So will you now take me, *ya talyeti, ya ghalyeti, ya noor donyeti,* all of me? Will you marry me and make me whole?"

Talia would have fallen if Harres hadn't caught her by the hips.

She stared down at him as he kneeled before her, shock and overwhelming joy twisting her tongue as she choked out, "Y-you're not—not promised to some m-marriage of state?

He smiled up at her, that annihilating smile that vaporized her mental functions at a hundred paces. "I'm not. I am free to marry the wife my heart chooses. And my heart, and everything in me, chooses you."

And she threw herself all over him, sobbing her love and relief. "Considering I'm yours forever, too, it's wise of you to make use of the fact."

From somewhere far away, she heard clapping and hooting.

Her infernal colleagues. They were still here?

Well, doctors in the E.R. didn't have much of a private life. She'd seen most of their revealing and embarrassing moments. They'd witnessed many of hers, too. Let them now share her most incredible one.

As she lost herself in Harres's fate-sealing kiss, one of her male colleagues said, "There's a very nice-size supply cabinet just around the corner, dude."

They both turned on him with a simultaneous, "Oh, shut *up.*"

Then, exchanging a conspiratorial look with Harres, she grabbed his hand and they rushed out of the room.

On their way out, a female colleague asked, "What if the Chief sees you signed in but nowhere around?"

"Tell him I have a gunshot victim to tend to," she said.

"Yes," Harres added. "Someone who's so impressed by her uncanny medical skills, he's going to donate any number of millions she sees fit to your department in gratitude."

They left the room to an explosion of excitement.

Once they reached that supply cabinet, he dragged her inside, pushed her against the wall. "And to this golden virago who owns my heart by awakening it, my life by saving it, my faith by inspiring it, what would you see fit I donate?"

She dragged him down to her, begged in his mouth. "Just your love. Just you."

And he pledged to her as he made her whole, "You have it, and me, always. Forever."

* * * * *

*Get swept away with
Olivia Gates's next passionate Silhouette Desire novel
THE SARANTOS SECRET BABY.*

*And don't miss the stunning conclusion
to the Pride of Zohayd trilogy, Amjad's story,
coming soon!*

COMING NEXT MONTH

Available March 8, 2011

REQUEST YOUR FREE BOOKS!

**2 FREE NOVELS
PLUS 2
FREE GIFTS!**

Passionate, Powerful, Provocative!

YES! Please send me 2 FREE Silhouette Desire® novels and my 2 FREE gifts (gifts are worth about $10). After receiving them, if I don't wish to receive any more books, I can return the shipping statement marked "cancel." If I don't cancel, I will receive 6 brand-new novels every month and be billed just $4.05 per book in the U.S. or $4.74 per book in Canada. That's a saving of at least 15% off the cover price! It's quite a bargain! Shipping and handling is just 50¢ per book in the U.S. and 75¢ per book in Canada.* I understand that accepting the 2 free books and gifts places me under no obligation to buy anything. I can always return a shipment and cancel at any time. Even if I never buy another book, the two free books and gifts are mine to keep forever.

225/326 SDN FC65

Name	(PLEASE PRINT)	
Address		Apt. #
City	State/Prov.	Zip/Postal Code

Signature (if under 18, a parent or guardian must sign)

Mail to the **Reader Service:**

IN U.S.A.: P.O. Box 1867, Buffalo, NY 14240-1867
IN CANADA: P.O. Box 609, Fort Erie, Ontario L2A 5X3

Not valid for current subscribers to Silhouette Desire books.

**Want to try two free books from another line?
Call 1-800-873-8635 or visit www.ReaderService.com.**

* Terms and prices subject to change without notice. Prices do not include applicable taxes. Sales tax applicable in N.Y. Canadian residents will be charged applicable taxes. Offer not valid in Quebec. This offer is limited to one order per household. All orders subject to credit approval. Credit or debit balances in a customer's account(s) may be offset by any other outstanding balance owed by or to the customer. Please allow 4 to 6 weeks for delivery. Offer available while quantities last.

Your Privacy—The Reader Service is committed to protecting your privacy. Our Privacy Policy is available online at www.ReaderService.com or upon request from the Reader Service.

We make a portion of our mailing list available to reputable third parties that offer products we believe may interest you. If you prefer that we not exchange your name with third parties, or if you wish to clarify or modify your communication preferences, please visit us at www.ReaderService.com/consumerschoice or write to us at Reader Service Preference Service, P.O. Box 9062, Buffalo, NY 14269. Include your complete name and address.

SDES11

USA TODAY *bestselling author Lynne Graham*
is back with a thrilling new trilogy
SECRETLY PREGNANT, CONVENIENTLY WED

Three heroines must marry alpha males to keep
their dreams…but Alejandro, Angelo and Cesario
are not about to be tamed!

Book 1—JEMIMA'S SECRET
Available March 2011 from Harlequin Presents®.

JEMIMA yanked open a drawer in the sideboard to find Alfie's birth certificate. Her son was her husband's child. It was a question of telling the truth whether she liked it or not. She extended the certificate to Alejandro.

"This has to be nonsense," Alejandro asserted.

"Well, if you can find some other way of explaining how I managed to give birth by that date and Alfie not be yours, I'd like to hear it," Jemima challenged.

Alejandro glanced up, golden eyes bright as blades and as dangerous. "All this proves is that you must still have been pregnant when you walked out on our marriage. It does not automatically follow that the child is mine."

"'I know it doesn't suit you to hear this news now and I really didn't want to tell you. But I can't lie to you about it. Someday Alfie may want to look you up and get acquainted."

"If what you have just told me is the truth, if that little boy does prove to be mine, it was vindictive and extremely selfish of you to leave me in ignorance!"

Jemima paled. "When I left you, I had no idea that I was still pregnant."

"Two years is a long period of time, yet you made no attempt to inform me that I might be a father. I will want DNA tests to confirm your claim before I make any decision about what I want to do."

"Do as you like," she told him curtly. "*I* know who Alfie's father is and there has never been any doubt of his identity."

"I will make arrangements for the tests to be carried out and I will see you again when the result is available," Alejandro drawled with lashings of dark Spanish masculine reserve.

"I'll contact a solicitor and start the divorce," Jemima proffered in turn.

Alejandro's eyes narrowed in a piercing scrutiny that made her uncomfortable. "It would be foolish to do anything before we have that DNA result."

"I disagree," Jemima flashed back. "I should have applied for a divorce the minute I left you!"

Alejandro quirked an ebony brow. "And why didn't you?"

Jemima dealt him a fulminating glance but said nothing, merely moving past him to open her front door in a blunt invitation for him to leave.

"I'll be in touch," he delivered on the doorstep.

What is Alejandro's next move? Perhaps rekindling their marriage is the only solution! But will Jemima agree?

*Find out in Lynne Graham's
exciting new romance
JEMIMA'S SECRET*

*Available March 2011
from Harlequin Presents®.*

Start your Best Body today with these top 3 nutrition tips!

1. **SHOP THE PERIMETER OF THE GROCERY STORE:** The good stuff—fruits, veggies, lean proteins and dairy—always line the outer edges of the store. When you veer into the center aisles, you enter the temptation zone, where the unhealthy foods live.

2. **WATCH PORTION SIZES:** Most portion sizes in restaurants are nearly twice the size of a true serving and at home, it's easy to "clean your plate." Use these easy serving guidelines:
   - Protein: the palm of your hand
   - Grains or Fruit: a cup of your hand
   - Veggies: the palm of two open hands

3. **USE THE RAINBOW RULE FOR PRODUCE:** Your produce drawers should be filled with every color of fruits and vegetables. The greater the variety, the more vitamins and other nutrients you add to your diet.

Find these and many more helpful tips in

YOUR BEST BODY NOW
by
TOSCA RENO
WITH STACY BAKER

Bestselling Author of
THE EAT-CLEAN DIET

Available wherever books are sold!

SAME GREAT STORIES AND AUTHORS!

Starting April 2011,
Silhouette Desire will become
Harlequin Desire, but rest assured
that this series will continue to be
the ultimate destination for Powerful,
Passionate and Provocative Romance
with the same great authors that
you've come to know and love!

♦ Harlequin®

Desire

ALWAYS POWERFUL, PASSIONATE
AND PROVOCATIVE

PRESENTING…THE SEVENTH ANNUAL
MORE THAN WORDS™ ANTHOLOGY

Five bestselling authors
Five real-life heroines

This year's Harlequin
More Than Words award
recipients have changed lives,
one good deed at a time. To
celebrate these real-life heroines,
some of Harlequin's most
acclaimed authors have honored
the winners by writing stories
inspired by these dedicated
women. Within the pages
of *More Than Words Volume 7*,
you will find novellas written
by Carly Phillips, Donna Hill
and Jill Shalvis—and online at
www.HarlequinMoreThanWords.com
you can also access stories by
Pamela Morsi and Meryl Sawyer.

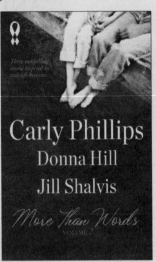

Coming soon in print and online!

Visit
www.HarlequinMoreThanWords.com
to access your FREE ebooks and to nominate
a real-life heroine in your community.

Proceeds from the sale of this book will be
reinvested in Harlequin's charitable initiatives.

MTWV7763CS